# ADE ADEPITAN

# CYBORG CAT

This edition published in Great Britain in 2019 by
Piccadilly Press
80-81 Wimpole St, London W1G 9RE

www.piccadillypress.co.uk

Text copyright © Ade Adepitan, 2018
Illustrations © Carl Pearce, 2019
Author photo © IWPHOTOGRAPHIC
With thanks to Ivor Baddiel

First published by Studio Press, 2018, as
*Ade's Amazing Ade-ventures: Battle of the Cyborg Cat*

A CIP catalogue record for this book is available from the
British Library.

ISBN: 978-1-848-12899-6

1 3 5 7 9 10 8 6 4 2

Typeset in OpenDyslexia-Alta by Perfect Bound Ltd

Printed and bound by Clays Ltd, Elcograf S.p.A.

MIX
Paper from
responsible sources
FSC
www.fsc.org   FSC® C018072

Piccadilly Press is an imprint of Bonnier Books,
www.bonnierbooks.co.uk

# ADE ADEPITAN

# CYBORG CAT

## RISE OF THE
## PARSONS ROAD GANG

Piccadilly PRESS

## The CYBORG CAT series

Rise of the Parsons Road Gang

Cyborg Cat and the Night Spider

*To my mum Christianah
and my late father Bola.
They helped nurture
my love of books and reading.*

**HEY,** how are you doing? My name is Adedoyin Olayiwola Adepitan. I know what you're thinking: That name must be worth a lot of points in a game of Scrabble! You'd be right. You may know me off the telly. I'm that guy who uses a wheelchair and is pretty good at basketball. I present quite a few shows, as well.

My family call me Doyin, which is the second part of my first name. My mum calls me by my full name, but only when I'm in trouble. Most of my friends call me Ade – not like the end of the word 'lemon-ade'.

And not like the letters 'A', 'D' and DEFINITELY NOT EDDIE! But more like the sound 'a' and the letter 'D'. Try it: Ah-dee! Got it.

This story is based on the time I moved to London with my family and started going to school here, in the 1980s. Okay, yeah, I know that's a long time ago (no need to be cheeky now).

The UK was very different back then; it was a time of interesting music, questionable fashion, severe haircuts (if you don't believe me, have a look at some of your mum and dad's old school pics) and, of course, it was when dad-dancing was invented...

Moving home can be pretty difficult. Moving to a completely different country to start a new life, well that's just scary. Especially when you realise that some people in your new neighbourhood might not like you because you look different to them. I'd had polio as a baby, so I also had to wear a heavy iron brace called a caliper on my left leg, and ugly-looking hospital boots, just so I could walk. Hospital boots: great for putting in a heavy tackle on the football pitch, terrible for dancing and absolutely impossible not to stick out like a sore thumb whenever you're wearing them!

But you know what? The caliper is why my friends started to call me Cyborg Cat. Don't know what a cyborg is? That's okay. Keep reading and you'll find out!

# 1

# Not a great breakfast

**THERE'S** never a good time to be
given bad news, but nine o'clock in the
morning, when you're hungrily shovelling
a large spoonful of Sugar Puffs and warm
milk into your mouth, is definitely one of the
worst times.

"Doyin, we're going to have a party to
celebrate our arrival in England," Mum said.
"It's been a few weeks now and we have a
lot to give thanks for."

Uh-oh. That did not sound good.

Mum and Dad love parties, but I knew what was coming.

I'd already put the cereal in my mouth, though, so, "Mmmm, whhuuummm dufff dooossshhhaaa," was the only response I could manage.

"Oh good. I know how much you like a party," Mum said. "I've invited all your cousins, aunties and uncles, and our family friends as well." She smiled. "We can all get dressed up."

This was what I was afraid of.

"No! No, we can't," I said, in a spray of Sugar Puffs. "People don't wear sokoto and agbada here."

Mum frowned. "Ade, it's a party. Our party. We need to look good. Anyway, I've already picked your outfit."

I groaned inwardly as I imagined myself in the traditional Nigerian dress: a pair of loose-fitting trousers and an oversized but ornate-looking shirt. They come in all sorts of patterns but my mum isn't interested in bland, boring styles. She has what you could call a very *interesting* dress sense, though another way of describing it might be an outrageous, completely over the top, what on earth is she thinking, dress sense. She always chooses the brightest and loudest colours for me to wear. But I could tell from her expression this was important to her.

"Okay, fine." I sighed. "Maybe I'll just stay inside. When is this party?" I was sure I could come up with an excuse to get out of it somehow.

"It's tomorrow," Mum said brightly.

Tomorrow! This was bad news. I wasn't at school yet, because we'd arrived from Nigeria during the summer holidays, so I didn't have any friends to get me out of it, and I couldn't even pretend to have urgent homework or something.

"Well, I guess it's just family anyway," I said.

Mum waved a hand. "Well, yes, family and also those young boys we saw playing football on our street last week."

The spoon slipped from my fingers. It clattered to the floor. This was a disaster.

"Mum! Why did you do that? We don't even know them!"

"Doyin." Mum was chuckling. I could tell that she thought I was over-reacting. "It's important for you to make new friends. You love playing football and so do they. Everything's going to be fine."

"It's not going to be fine!" I shouted, my cheeks getting hot and my eyes suddenly stinging with tears. "They're going to think I'm weird and laugh at me."

Before Mum could say anything else, I got down from the table, thudded up to my room and slammed the door shut.

I threw myself onto my bed and buried my face in my pillow. Mum just didn't get it.

Ever since we'd arrived in London, I'd decided that the best thing I could do was to keep as quiet as possible and not draw any attention to myself. If no one can see you or hear you, then they can't be nasty to you. I'd decided I'd just stay in my room with my action figures and X-Men comics all summer. And if I did have to leave the house I'd wear a hat and make sure my caliper was covered up.

You see, I am quite small for an almost ten-year-old, I suppose, but that's not the only different thing about me. I wear a metal support on my left leg, because I had polio when I was a baby so it makes me walk with a bit of a limp.

Anyway, in Nigeria it hadn't seemed to matter too much, but when we arrived in England a few weeks ago I realised how different we looked from all the other families.

My plan had been working well so far, but parties are big and noisy and full of people, which was exactly the sort of thing that would draw attention to our family.

And Nigerian parties are the biggest and the noisiest of them all.

I heard footsteps on the stairs and quickly dived under the covers so no one could see me crying.

"Hmm, I wonder where Doyin could be?" Mum said as the door clicked open.

I lay as still as I could.

"Oh well," Mum went on, "I'll just have to sit on the end of the bed. Sit RIGHT HERE and wait till he comes back."

What? I didn't fancy getting squished beneath Mum's bottom so I swiftly crawled up through the blankets and emerged into the daylight.

"Oh, there you are, Doyin." Mum sat down next to me and gave me a hug.

I hugged her back, snivelling and feeling a little embarrassed. My tears had taken me by surprise.

Mum gently kissed my forehead and said softly, "Don't cry, Doyin. Why do you think those boys would laugh at you?"

*Because my caliper makes me look like C3PO from Star Wars but with chewing gum stuck to the bottom of my left foot,* I thought.

I didn't say that, though. I didn't want to upset her.

"Maybe because of my caliper?"

Mum shook her head. "When they see how talented, intelligent and handsome you are they will love you, not laugh at you."

She pinched my cheeks and stared down at me with her big bright eyes. Mum has a

way of making you feel better with one look,
but I still didn't believe her.

This party was going to be a disaster.

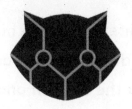

# 2
# Plans A, B, C and D

**MUM** was cooking all last night, and all this morning. She even sent Dad out for more ingredients. Sitting here at the kitchen table, sniffing the air, I could tell she was cooking all my favourite dishes: fried plantain, chicken and my much-loved moi moi – a steamed bean pudding that has no business tasting as good as it does, considering it's made of beans! This much food means an awful lot of people. Including the boys from the street.

This is definitely going to be a disaster.

"Oh, Doyin, don't look so sad." Dad staggered into the kitchen and put down the heavy shopping. "Do you want some jelly?"

Before I had a chance to react, Dad swept me up into the air and onto my back on the kitchen floor.

"No, Dad, not the jelly hands," I squealed. Dad can make his hands go all wobbly like jelly when he tickles. But it was too late.

I laughed until tears ran down my cheeks. Afterwards, when Dad got tired and lay next to me on the floor, I started thinking about the party again. I could feel knots tightening in my stomach.

Then Dad went and made things even worse. "I can't wait for the party to start." He jumped to his feet. "I'm going to show everyone my best dance moves!"

I looked at Mum. We both knew what was coming next.

"Oh yeah, who's the daddy?" Dad said as he moved to the centre of the room. He started making weird high-pitched noises, stamping his feet and flailing his arms about wildly in what he probably thinks are some of his best dance moves, but, by anyone else's standards, would probably be their worst.

As Dad gyrated, he clattered into some pots and pans. Then he bumped into a chair. Almost in one motion, whilst his bottom landed on the seat, he placed his right leg over his left and sat upright, folding his arms. He gave me and Mum a knowing look, like falling onto the chair was part of the move.

He nearly pulled it off, as well. Then a saucepan that had been resting precariously on the shelf behind him wobbled and fell off. It landed on the top of Dad's neatly combed Afro with a ...

**BONG.**

I covered my face with my hands. There's only one thing for it, I thought. I *have* to get this party cancelled.

"I see, sir. So you would like one hundred mice delivered to your house this afternoon?"

I was on the phone to the local pet shop, Petty Minded. I'd found their number in something called *The Phone Book*, which was basically the biggest book in the world, full of page after page after page of phone numbers. I don't know why anyone would want to read a book like that, but on page 1437 I'd found the number of the pet shop and dialled it.

My idea was simple, and genius: scatter the mice all over the house. Mum and Dad would think that all the food they'd been cooking had attracted them and they were now overrun with the creatures. No one would want to come to a house infested with mice, so they'd *definitely* have to cancel the party.

I'd put on the deepest voice I could. So far it seemed to be working.

"Yes, that's right," I said. "One hundred mice, please."

"Very good," said the man. "Could I take an address for the delivery?"

"I live at 4 Parsons Road in Plaistow." My parents had made me learn the address off by heart almost as soon as we'd moved in, just in case I ever got lost and had to tell someone where I lived.

"Thank you, sir," said the man. "So that's one hundred mice, plus delivery charge. That will be forty pounds exactly. Will that be cash or cheque?"

Uh-oh. There was a major flaw in my otherwise perfect plan. I have no money.

"Erm, I, erm, I've changed my mind," I said

quickly. "And I need to go to the toilet. Bye."

I slammed the phone down quickly and shook my head. Nice work. Especially the toilet detail. Nope, I don't think I'll be visiting Petty Minded any time soon. Or ever, for that matter.

Luckily, my second plan was much simpler and, most importantly, didn't involve me having to phone anyone or spend any money.

You can't have a party without music.

So all I had to do was get rid of all my parents' records. Easy-peasy. Just don't get caught. I'd be like a cat burglar trying to steal the Crown Jewels.

Very quietly and very slowly, I crept downstairs and into the front room. I could hear Mum and Dad in the kitchen, chatting and joking, which was actually very helpful. Dad has a really loud voice, so they were even less likely to hear me.

I stopped in front of my parents' record collection. There seemed to be a lot more records than I'd remembered. I'd planned to take them up to my room one by one, and then hide them under my bed, but the party would be over before I'd removed half of them.

I shrugged. I'd just need to speed it up. I grabbed a bunch of records and sneaked out of the room as quietly as I could. I was halfway up the stairs when three of the records escaped from their sleeves and made a run for it.

Two of the records flopped down a couple of steps and stopped. The third record had other ideas. Big ideas. It bounced down all the steps like a spinning wheel then carried on along the corridor.

Uh-oh.

"Come back. Please."

But the record didn't listen. It went straight

through the door and into the kitchen.

I dropped the other records and as quickly as I could climbed the stairs back to my room.

I'd just closed the door when I heard Dad shouting my name.

"Adedoyin Olayiwola Adepitan!"

Third time lucky, right?

I stood on the landing and listened to Mum and Dad go out into the garden to put out chairs. My next plan was so simple I couldn't believe I hadn't thought of it to begin with.

If no one can find the house, there won't be a party. So all I need to do is get rid of the door number.

I threw Dad's tool belt over my shoulder and crept down the stairs. I gently flicked the latch on the door and went outside. There, by the side of the door, was the number 4. All I had to do was take it off the wall and no one would know where 4 Parsons Road was. Job done.

I plucked a screwdriver from the belt. It had a flat head, and the screws attaching the number to the wall had a cross in them, but surely that wouldn't be a problem? A screwdriver is a screwdriver.

I could just about reach the top screw. I stretched up, put the bright red screwdriver in and turned.

Nothing.

I grabbed the screwdriver with both hands and really turned.

Nothing.

I jiggled the screwdriver this way and that to try to loosen the screw.

Nothing.

I got the green hammer out of the belt and hammered the screwdriver in as much as I could, and then turned.

Nothing.

It was hopeless.

I trudged back up to my room, undid the straps on my caliper, crawled under the covers of my bed and curled up into a ball.

This was plan number four. Stay in bed. Maybe everyone will forget about me. Maybe I'm a superhero who can make myself disappear.

But I'd forgotten. Superheroes didn't look like me. Those men in the market had made sure I understood that.

**QUEEN'S MARKET E13**

BOROUGH OF NEWHAM

# 3
# Queen's Market

**"OI,** why don't you go back to your own country and take the little cripple boy with you?"

Those were the first words anyone had said to me and my parents since we had left the airport. In fact, if you ignored the customs officer who only grunted hello, and the police officer who pointed to where the train station was, those were the first words any British person had ever said to us.

"Don't take any notice, Doyin," Dad had muttered.

Mum's jaw was tight. "Just keep walking." She'd glanced over her shoulder. "Quickly. Keep walking. Quickly."

Dad didn't hesitate; he scooped me up and put me on his shoulders. Then he picked up the suitcase once more and strode on.

Okay, so I'm small for a nine-year-old. But still.

"Wait! I wanted to walk –"

Dad just tightened his grip on me. The metal of my caliper give a little squeak of protest. It was as if it was also warning me to be quiet. It seemed to be saying, *There's danger nearby, shhh.*

I looked down at Mum and saw that she had moved in closer to Dad.

We strode on, past a few market stalls, my parents keeping their heads down. I caught a glimpse of a sign that read Queen's

Market and I could hear the call of traders.

The colour, chaos, hustle and bustle of the busy market didn't seem all that different to markets back home in Nigeria selling everything from fruit, to fish, to trousers – though here they called them farahs. If I hadn't heard that mean, angry voice behind us, I'd have been thinking how easy it would be in this new country. But I did hear that voice.

As we came alongside a stall selling bottles promising 'the ultimate shine for your bathroom', a group of men barged past. There were four of them in total and they stood in a line, blocking the way ahead. They all had very short hair and were wearing white T-shirts, braces, jeans and green jackets with Union Jack flags on them.

The shortest one looked the meanest. He stared at us with bloodshot eyes and a smell rolled off him that made my nose sting. It reminded me of Uncle Lanre coming back from a big party. I hated that smell. It was so strong that without thinking I put my finger under my nose to stop it.

The short man didn't like that and spat on the floor right by Dad's feet.

"Please," said Dad. "We don't want any trouble. We just want to get to our house."

"Yeah, well we don't want you or your type here," shouted one of the other men. "So go back to your house in Bongo Bongo Land."

They all laughed at that, but it wasn't a funny, happy laugh. They sounded like dogs being strangled.

I thought it was a weird thing to say. Where's Bongo Bongo Land? Had Mum and Dad bought a house there without telling me?

"And we don't want stupid cripples here, either," said the man at the front.

Stupid cripple?

I tried to get my head around that. Yes, I wear a caliper that supports my leg but that doesn't make me a cripple and it doesn't make me stupid.

The men scared me, but I had to say something. Why do these men, who've never met me before, think I'm stupid?

Mum was quicker than me, though. She stepped forwards and looked right into the man's bloodshot eyes and shouted, "My son is not stupid, and he is not a cripple!"

Mum's back was as straight as a ruler and she was so angry she was shaking. Back home, when Mum got angry people were scared of her, but that wasn't happening with these men. They just seemed to think it was very funny and started laughing those horrible laughs again.

The market around us had fallen silent. There was no more hustle and bustle. The other market traders and shoppers were all looking in our direction. All those eyes watching us made me feel like we were on display.

I looked around and my gaze locked with one of the traders, a big man wearing a funny-looking checked hat. He looked upset.

*Help us.* My heart was beating so fast I thought it might burst out of my chest.

The trader took a step forwards, but one of the men, the tallest one, screwed up his face and pointed a finger towards the guy's face. "Don't even think about it!" he snarled.

The trader and everybody around him quickly looked away and then carried on as if nothing had happened.

No one was going to help us. I didn't think it was possible, but my heart started to beat even faster.

The four men laughed again, but a moment later they stopped and the one at the front with the smelly breath looked at

Dad, his eyes full of hatred and menace.

"Right," he said. "I'm going to give you five seconds to turn round and get out of here." He patted his jacket pocket. "Or else."

"One."

"Two."

"Come on." Mum's voice trembled. "We'll find another way."

"Three."

Mum tugged on Dad's arm. "Come on, Bola."

"Four."

Dad stared at the man, refusing to look away. Then, "We're going," he said.

We turned around and walked out of the market the way we'd come, the sound of the men's laughter still ringing in my ears.

# 4
# The party

**"DOYIN!** DOYIN! Come down. Everyone wants to see you."

I don't know how many hours I'd spent sulking beneath the sheets since my plans had failed, but now the celebrations had begun and it was clear that this party was probably going to be the loudest that Parsons Road had ever seen. So much for my plan of staying under the radar.

Uncle Sobanjo was first to arrive with his speakers and amplifier, and before long I heard the familiar rhythmic drums, melodic guitar and hypnotic vocals of King Sunny Ade, one of Dad's favourite artists. Soon, the whole house seemed to be dancing to the rhythm.

"Now, Doyin!" Mum yelled.

Uh-oh. What if she comes up and carries me down? What if the boys from the street see?

I've got no choice.

I took a deep breath, pulled the sheets back and got myself ready to go downstairs. Time to face the music. I buckled the straps of my caliper around my left thigh and then my knee. Then I put on my sokoto and agbada, which were white with blue, orange and red swirly patterns dotted all over them, and took one last look in the mirror.

The iron rods from my caliper were showing. The rods end in a tiny 'L' shape and slot into holes in the heel of the hospital boot on my left leg. I usually cover them as best I can, but it isn't much good. It's obvious that I'm wearing something strange on my leg; there's just no hiding it.

I took another deep breath and headed down the stairs and into the hallway. The party was a sea of people flowing through the house.

Uncles, aunties, cousins and family friends, all with huge smiles on their faces, swooped down on me. Their warm hugs and compliments about how nice I looked relaxed me a little but I couldn't help scanning the surroundings. Where were the boys that Mum invited?

Suddenly the knots in my stomach were gone. They're not coming! Of course they're not!

I grinned, grabbed some food and went into the front room where everyone was dancing.

Munching on a chicken drumstick, I watched one of my cousins dancing. It looked like fun, and I was just about to join her when I spotted something through the window.

Oh no.

The three boys who played football on Parsons Road were standing right in front of our house. There were two teenagers with them, a stocky boy and a tall girl, who I didn't recognise.

As I stared at them, the girl suddenly started laughing and pointed down the street. My chest tightened.

Walking towards our house was my auntie and uncle, Mr and Mrs Okolie. They looked fantastic in their traditional Nigerian clothes, but obviously the older boy and girl didn't think so.

As my uncle and aunt got closer, the older boy began making grunting noises and scratching under his armpits. Then he started hopping up and down from one foot to the other. The girl thought this was really funny and laughed even harder.

"Go home monkeys!" she shouted in between fits of giggles. "Ooo-ooo-ooo."

The younger boys didn't join in with the laughter or the mockery. The three of them just looked at their feet.

My heart started pounding hard. I was back in Queen's Market facing those horrible men. The same thing seemed to be happening again, only this time it was on our street, where we'd made our home.

Why are there so many angry people in this country? Maybe I'll get angry as well.

My hands curled into fists as I marched to the front door. I yanked it open just as my aunt and uncle arrived.

Uncle had his arms around his wife as if he was trying to protect her from the teenagers' words. I could see the sadness on

Auntie's face, but as soon as she saw me her eyes lit up.

"This is the young man we've come to see." She gave me a huge hug. "Look how much you've grown."

Uncle smiled and shook my hand. "How are you, Doyin?" he asked.

"I'm fine, Uncle," I said, looking down the path at the kids standing outside the front garden. The girl and the boy were still chuckling. "Please come in. Mum and Dad can't wait to see you."

Auntie and Uncle smiled and made their way into the house while I stared at the kids. Fear was fighting with anger. Five against one was not good odds if things turned nasty. But I couldn't keep quiet, not this time.

I gritted my teeth and strode to the front gate, not caring that I was wearing Nigerian clothes and that everyone could see my caliper.

"What do you want?" the tall girl snarled.

"Yeah. Go back to your monkeys' tea party, Peg Leg!" the older boy shouted.

"Why don't you shut your stupid fat mouth!" Anger made my voice much louder than I'd expected and once I started, I couldn't stop. "I've seen real monkeys and they're amazing and intelligent creatures, unlike you and your stupid friends!"

There was a stunned silence. The boy's mouth opened and closed like a fish. His hands curled into fists as he stared at me.

I was shaking. My heart was pounding so hard it felt like it was trying to escape my chest.

He's going to punch me. It's going to hurt.

**PARSONS ROAD** E13

BOROUGH OF NEWHAM

# 5

# The Parsons Road Gang

**THE** teenager took a step forwards, fist raised, but then a voice stopped him.

"Do you know what the difference is between monkeys and apes?" the voice said.

It came from a tall, skinny boy wearing blue-rimmed glasses. He had Afro hair shaped into a box cut, which made him look even taller. He came to stand next to me but didn't wait for an answer to his question and continued as if he were a teacher giving a lesson.

33

"Monkeys have tails and apes don't, and the whole of the human race evolved from apes, hundreds of thousands of years ago," he said.

I blinked. I was unsure quite what to make of this development.

The teenagers frowned. "Shut up, Brian," said the boy. "You and Peg Leg may be monkeys, but we're not."

The girl nodded. "Let's go before we're bored to death. We'll leave Monkey Boy and Four Eyes to it. Come on, you lot."

The teenagers turned to leave, but the other boys stayed where they were.

"Nah, you're alright," said the small boy with bright ginger hair. "We're gonna stay right here with Brian."

The boy next to him, who was as wide as he was tall, nodded.

"Fine. Suit yourselves," the teenager replied. "Come on, Sam, I've got better things to do than waste my time talking to these mugs!"

The two teenagers walked off, making monkey sounds as they went.

I narrowed my eyes as I watched them go, then turned to the three boys still stood by my house. Why had they stayed? Did they want trouble?

I looked each of the kids in the eye, daring them to say something. It reminded me of a western I'd watched with Dad. The first person to flinch or back down loses, and it wasn't going to be me.

The boy with the blue-rimmed glasses stuck out a welcoming hand.

"I'm Brian. I'm the brains around here, but you probably guessed that."

I shook his hand. "Hi," I said, trying to make my voice sound deeper. "My name's Ade."

"Don't listen to Brian, Ade!" shouted the boy with ginger hair. "He only thinks he's the brains. I'm Dexter Trimmingham the Third. I've got the best right foot in East London."

To prove his point, Dexter swung his right foot wildly in my direction as if he were blasting a football past me.

"I'm Shezhad," mumbled the last boy. "But everyone calls me Shed."

I looked Shed up and down. He really was huge.

"Sorry about my cousin." Dexter shuffled from side to side. "Deano's not always like that, honestly. Sometimes he's really nice."

"Oh yeah, like that time he helped those ants sunbathe by using a magnifying glass." Brian rolled his eyes.

Shed chuckled to himself then looked away because everyone had turned to look at him.

"Shut it, Brian." Dexter's face was turning apple red. "You know his family are going through a tough time."

Time to change the subject, clearly. "Who's the girl?" I asked.

"Samantha Pringle," said Dexter. "She's Deano's girlfriend. Deano's only just turned thirteen, but she's fourteen and she –"

Dexter broke off as Mum came rushing out of the house.

"Are you okay, Doyin?" she said, slightly out of breath. "Your auntie said you came out here on your own."

I looked at the three boys. They all seemed a little confused and I thought I knew why.

"My full name's Adedoyin," I explained. "Some people call me Doyin, not Ade."

"Oh!" they said as one.

"I'm fine, Mum," I told her. I kind of wished she'd go inside. Having just stood up to Deano and Sam on my own, the last thing I wanted the others to think was that I only did it because Mum would come out to help me.

Dexter stepped forwards and said, "Hi, Ade's mum, I'm Dexter Trimmingham the Third, and these are my friends Brian and Shed."

"Pleased to meet you all," Mum replied. "But what are you doing out here?"

"Oh, well, you see, you invited us." Brian pushed his glasses up his nose. "Didn't you?"

Mum laughed. "What I mean is, don't stand out here, come inside and have something to eat. We've got chicken, plantain and jollof rice – it's only a little spicy."

I gaped at her. A *little bit spicy!?* The jollof rice was my cousin's speciality and Dad called it dragon fuel. The last time I tried some I'd had to sit for two hours with ice cubes in my mouth. What if one of the boys combusted from eating the food? I could see the headlines in the papers:

# *DEATH BY JOLLOF!*

## Three young British boys explode after eating Cousin Remi's fiery jollof rice.

Thankfully, when we got inside my fears were unfounded. Brian, Dexter and Shed witnessed another of my cousins rushing to the kitchen to drink fifteen glasses of water, in agony after one spoonful of the rice.

They tucked into the chicken and plantain instead and couldn't get enough of it.

"Great party!" all three of them said in unison.

"Thank you." I'd been so worried about them coming but it was actually okay. Things seem much worse when you're imagining them, I guess. But when you confront the reality, it's really not that bad at all.

"What are those clothes you're wearing?" Dexter asked, breaking into my thoughts.

So this was exactly the sort of question I'd been dreading earlier in the day. I decided to be up front and proud. "They're traditional Nigerian clothes."

Dexter looked intrigued. "Where's Nigeria?" he asked.

"Well, you take a left after Queen's Market," I began. "Then head up Green Street and it's just next to the pie 'n' mash shop."

Dexter scratched his head, trying to work out if he'd seen this mysterious place called Nigeria.

Brian laughed. "Nigeria is in West Africa, Dex, you silly sausage!"

Dexter screwed up his eyes. "I knew that, I'm not stupid!" Then, a moment later, he said, "Where's Africa?"

This time when Shed and Brian started laughing I joined in too.

Shed pointed to my leg and the metal rods going into my boot. "So, are you a robot or something?" he asked.

I opened my mouth to explain that I'd had polio as a baby and it had made my muscles weak and how the caliper supported my left leg so I could walk. But before I could say anything ...

"Obviously, he's a robot!" Dexter said. He started making strange mechanical noises and walking stiffly down the corridor with his arms rigid by his sides.

Shed chuckled as Dexter pretended he was a malfunctioning robot and bumped into the wall.

"WHO PUT THIS HERE? DESTROY, DESTROY!"

Dexter sounded just like a dalek from *Doctor Who*.

Brian put down his plate of food. "He's not a robot, he's a cyborg!"

"Am I?" What was a cyborg, anyway?

"Yeah, so a cyborg is a human with mechanical enhancements that give them super-strength," Brian said knowingly. I was getting the feeling Brian knew quite a lot.

"AWESOME!" said Dexter.

"Super-strength," I said. "Sounds good to me."

"That means you can play football, right?" Shed asked.

"Of course I can!" I turned to Dexter, grinned and said cheekily, "I've got the best left foot in East London."

Shed nudged Brian and gave him a look as if he wanted him to say something. But before Brian could say a word, Dexter stepped forwards and announced, "We're the Parsons Road Gang. We don't cause trouble, we just love playing football and we could do with a player with super-cyborg-strength. Wanna join our team?"

Suddenly I felt tingly with happiness. It was as if my caliper was sort of ... glowing. It felt like it was giving me power, somehow. I told myself to be cool. "Yeah, I'll join your team."

"Great," said Brian. "We'll call for you tomorrow morning, Ade. We can work on our skills."

Tomorrow seemed a long time to wait to play football.

"Hey, why are we waiting?" I said. "Let's play in my garden."

"What, now?" asked Brian.

"Yes," I said. "Right now."

# 6
# Super-Strength

**THE** great thing about football is that if you've got a ball you don't really need much else. In fact, sometimes you don't even need a ball. I've played many matches with a scrunched-up piece of paper and even a plastic cup.

Thankfully, though, this time I did have a ball. A pretty cool one, too. It was already outside in the small back garden. Dad bought it for me from a shop in Upton Park.

"Whoa! Is that a West Ham football?"

Brian's eyes were wide as he spotted the claret-and-blue football.

"It's a real-life, actual Mitre Pro 2000!" Dexter charged forwards, the ball a magnet that couldn't be resisted.

We all chased after him. I knew I wasn't as quick as my new friends. The caliper is heavy and slows me down and the iron rods mean I can't bend my left leg either, which means I can't move in the same way as the others. But it's never stopped me before. And it wasn't going to stop me now.

As the game went on, I noticed Shed looking at me. He was watching my heavy limp and how I favour my right side because I've got more strength there.

*He thinks I can't keep up.* I tried to push away my annoyance, but when Shed passed the ball to me with the feeblest cross ever, I knew I had to say something.

People don't understand things they

haven't seen before. To my friends and family in Nigeria I'm just plain old Ade. But Shed, Brian and Dexter have obviously never seen anybody like me. As well as my leg, I'm dressed differently and I suppose I've got a strange accent compared to their East London voices.

As the ball Shed kicked trickled slowly over to me, I knew this would be the first of many tests. All I really wanted was to be like everybody else and fit in, but to do that I'd have to prove I wasn't any different from the other kids. I'd have to show them.

I maneuvered myself so the ball came towards my strong right foot. Then I blasted it as hard as I could towards Dexter. As the ball flew towards him like an arrow, Dexter just had time to open his mouth in amazement before it hit him on the forehead and then spun off in the air.

"**TIIIMBEEER!**" Brian yelled.

Dexter fell to the ground with his arms open wide.

"Sorry, mate!" I yelled as the rest of the boys cracked up.

We finally managed to stop laughing but it was hard because Dexter was now pretending to be dazed and walking around in dizzy circles.

Shed shook his head. "Amazing shot."

Brian came over and put his arm around my shoulders. He looked at Shed and Dexter and said, "I told you he had super-strength." He said 'super-strength' slowly and quietly as if it was their secret.

"Ah! Shut up!" I said, trying to hide my smile. "Come on, let's play football."

Shed looked at me. Then we both raced towards the ball, which was at the far end of the garden. Shed got to it first. He tried to dribble past me, but I called on my super-strength and slid into him with a crunching tackle. We both fell to the ground in a heap.

Brian and Dexter jumped on top of us in a classic bundle. I ended up underneath Shed and was laughing so hard it took me a minute to realise that someone was shouting my name.

"DOYIN! DOYIN!"

Uh-oh, Mum.

"Adedoyin Olayiwola Adepitan!" she shouted again. "What are you doing? Your agbada and sokoto are going to get filthy!"

The boys rolled off me quick-fast.

I sat up and brushed down my outfit. The mud wasn't budging.

Mum shook her head.

"I think it's time for us to go." Brian got to his feet.

Dexter nodded. "Yeah, my mum will be expecting me."

My new friends were leaving. I wished they wouldn't. I slowly started to stand up and as I did so, a big hand grabbed my arm and helped me to my feet. It was Shed.

"Great tackle," he said, smiling.

I grinned back. It made me feel good.

We all headed back into the house and towards the front door, passing the living room where Dad had just moved to the centre. The beat kicked in and a loud whoop came from Dad.

"Come on, everybody, give me some space. Let me show you amateurs how it's done!"

With all the aunties and uncles clapping and cheering, he started pointing at them and gyrating as if he were being electrocuted, before screaming at the top of his voice, "Hee! Hee! Oh yeah, now that's how we do it in Lagos."

I stared at Dad in horror and then at my new friends. Brian, Dexter and Shed were transfixed. I felt sick. Dad was going to ruin everything with his crazy dance moves. What if he attempts the Worm? It'll be a disaster.

Brian turned to me. "My dad does that as well," he sighed. "Loves doing the Funky Chicken. It's terrible."

I laughed, mainly out of relief. I didn't know what the Funky Chicken was, but everyone knows chickens can't dance.

"We'll see you tomorrow." Dexter waved as he headed off on the short journey to his house.

"Yeah, see you tomorrow, Ade," said Brian and Shed, walking in the opposite direction. They live next to each other, two doors up from our house.

As I shut the door my face ached from smiling so much. Then the phone rang in the hallway. Mum answered it.

"How many mice?" she asked. "A hundred?!"

I could feel Mum's glare boring into

my back as I rushed into the front room, planning to lose myself in the crowd.

"Hey, Dad," I shouted. "Make room for me. Let's do the Worm!"

# 7

# Football, football and more football

"**SLOW** down," Mum said. "You'll give yourself indigestion eating your breakfast so fast."

I stuffed some more toast in my mouth and strained to listen for the doorbell. What if I missed Dexter, Shed and Brian calling? They might think I've changed my mind, about everything – playing football, joining the Parsons Road Gang, being their friend. They'll head off without me and never invite me to play with them again.

I swallowed the last bite of toast and ran to the window. There was still no sign of them, so I headed up to my bedroom and paced around. All sorts of other thoughts started running through my head. Maybe they'd decided I was just too strange to have as a friend: the way I walk, my accent, my crazy family. Even though they'd had great fun at the party, after having had some time to think about it they probably don't want to have anything to do with me anymo—

**DING DONG!**

I raced out of my room and slid down the banisters. (Sliding down the banisters is something I've perfected since being in England.) I landed at the bottom of the stairs just before Mum, who was also heading to the door.

"It's okay, I've got this," I panted, slightly out of breath.

Mum gave me a disapproving frown. She's probably still upset about how quickly I ate breakfast ... oh, and the mice. That had been tricky to explain.

I opened the door to find Dexter, Shed and Brian standing in the front garden, all with cheesy grins on their faces.

"Are you coming out or what?" Dexter sounded impatient.

Using his index finger, Brian pushed his blue-rimmed glasses from the end of his nose back up his face. He smiled. "It's time to see how good you really are, Ade."

"As long as he doesn't celebrate scoring goals by dancing like his dad we'll be okay," Shed chipped in.

"Cyborgs don't dance, they just win," I replied. "Come on, let's go."

The boys all laughed and ran onto Parsons Road.

It was hot. They were wearing shorts

and football tops. I wasn't. Even though it was very warm, I didn't really want the others to see the caliper on my leg, so I was wearing a pair of bright blue tracksuit bottoms. Cyborg or not, I still felt a little self-conscious.

The others didn't seem to have noticed, though, or if they had they weren't saying anything. Anyway, it didn't take long before I totally forgot about my caliper and just started having fun.

We played all day and then, the next morning, we did it all over again. And then the next day and the next.

Out on the pitch, I was okay. I'm a pretty good passer, and I'm a demon tackler, but I do struggle with running. But when I'm in goal, everything changes. I can catch and save anything that comes at me, even from close range. It's like my caliper gives me strength. I'm totally fearless!

"You know what?" Brian said one afternoon. "I'm not going to call you Ade or Doyin any more. You're Cyborg Cat."

"Cyborg Cat?" Ade repeated.

"Yeah," Dexter said. "Because you have the reflexes of a cat. It's one of your superpowers."

I grinned. I love superheroes. I love that my friends think I am one.

I'd actually needed superpowers for the length of the game we'd just played. It had ended 108–107, though no one was quite sure if that

was right as we'd sort of lost count after goal number 100.

We all lay on our backs on the pavement having a rest. This was the best summer of my life. The horrible men in Queen's Market seemed a long time ago now, even though the memory of that day does creep up on me sometimes. But I'm not the same scared little boy who shut myself away from the world before I met the Parsons Road Gang.

"Oi!" a deep voice yelled.

I felt a surge of fear. All the happy feelings disappeared. I sat up.

"Look what you've done to my tomatoes!" It was Mr Smoothhead from up the road. He pointed a finger at us. "Next time I see that ball in my garden I'll put a hole in it the size of the Blackwall Tunnel, you little bleeders!"

"Sorry," we said as one.

Dexter pulled us into a huddle. "Listen. There's a place, a secret place, where we can play football on proper grass with proper goal posts, and away from grumps like Mr Smoothhead. My brother told me about it the other day."

"So why are you just telling us now?" Brian demanded.

Dexter glanced at my caliper. "It's a bit too far to walk. We'd have to go there on our bikes."

I sighed deeply. "Well that's no good for me, is it?"

The other three looked at me. I could tell they were embarrassed. They thought I was going to say something about my leg. I decided I'd better put them out of their misery.

"I don't have a bike!"

Dexter punched me on the shoulder. "Joker."

Shed grinned. "No problem, you can jump on the back of mine."

"Great," I said. "Problem solved. Tomorrow we'll saddle up and head off to the secret football pitch."

# 8
# Silly sausages and broken dreams

**MY** friends arrived even earlier than usual the next morning. Shed was on his bright red three-speed Raleigh Chopper, Dexter had a chrome BMX Diamondback and Brian had a blue six-speed racing bike.

"Ready?" Shed asked.

I nodded and climbed onto the back of Shed's Chopper. My caliper scraped against the back wheel of the bike, even though it was covered up by my tracksuit bottoms. I tried to ignore it. "Come on, let's go!"

"Wait a second," Brian said. "You definitely got the sausages, Dex?"

"Yep, sausages packed." Dexter pushed down hard on his pedals and set off, followed by Brian.

"Why do we need to bring sausages?"

Shed shrugged. "I guess we'll find out." He pedalled after the other two.

I held on tight and watched the houses on Parsons Road fly by. There were snapshots of scenes that now felt familiar and comforting: kids playing out front, Dexter's older brother with his mates trying to fix up a car, women on the front step talking about what was on TV last night. Then ...

**Woof, woof... grrr... woof... woof.**

That sound was not familiar or comforting.

I looked behind us to see a huge German Shepherd leap over a garden wall and start to chase us.

"IT'S KING!" Dexter cried. "See, Brian, I told you he was big."

Brian quickly glanced back. "Whoa, that dog's huge!" His feet and the pedals became a blur.

"Faster, faster!" I screamed. I'm no fool. Sitting on the back of Shed's bike meant I'd be King's first course if the dog caught up with us.

Shed stood up and pedalled even harder to try to get away.

"Sausages!" he screamed as we whizzed past Dexter, who'd slowed right down.

"I'm trying," Dexter cried, his fingers fumbling about in his coat pocket. King was directly behind him now, teeth gnashing.

**"THROW THE SAUSAGES, YOU SILLY SAUSAGE!"** Brian yelled from the front.

*If I really was Cyborg Cat I could pluck Dexter from his bike and bound to safety.*

But Dexter didn't need a superhero. He

needed a distraction. Pulling a string of raw, fat Wall's sausages from his pocket, he hurled them at the dog. They soared through the air like some sort of weird flying caterpillar and were caught about six feet from the ground by the ravenous creature. With a yelp of pleasure, King completely forgot about us and greedily chomped down on the sausages.

'Woo hoo! Nice work, Dexter!" I yelled.

"Talk about leaving it to the last minute," Brian reprimanded from the front.

"Rubbish," said Dexter. "I had the situation under complete control. Come on!"

He took the lead once more and we zoomed forwards, only stopping once we arrived at a place called Southern Road Playing Fields.

It was just as Dexter had described it – a full-size football pitch with huge goals and beautiful well-cut and well-maintained grass. Even the markings on the pitch looked beautiful. I couldn't wait to put a ball on the bright white penalty spot and take a shot at goal.

"Why isn't anyone else here?" I asked.

"A local team used to play on the pitch," Dexter explained, "but they went bankrupt and had to leave. The caretaker, Mr James, loves his job, though, so he keeps it in good condition."

"But doesn't he mind when people use it?" asked Shed.

"Nah," said Dexter. "He told my brother he's fine with people using it as long as there's no litter and no trouble."

"Oi, stop yakking, you two," shouted Brian, moving along the fence to a hole big enough for them to get through. "It's time for kick-off."

We played all morning and then flopped down on the grass to wolf down lunch.

"Let's have another penalty competition after this," said Dexter in between bites of peanut butter sandwich.

"Waste of time," said Shed. "I'll only win again."

"Not a chance," snorted Brian. "You only won before because Dex burped and put me off on my last penalty."

"So how come you missed the other three before that?" Shed replied, laughing.

"Listen," I interjected. "None of you are going to win, because I'm going to save every single one of your penalties."

"Yeah?" said Dexter. "We'll see about that."

Everyone dropped their sandwiches. It was clearly time for the rematch.

I got in goal. Brian went first and scored three of his five penalties, followed by Dexter, who scored three as well.

I was hurling myself through the air as if

I was playing on marshmallows rather than grass. I was loving it, despite the fact that the goals were gigantic compared to me. I was pulling off some spectacular saves.

Now the pressure was all on Shed. He put the ball on the penalty spot and stepped back what seemed like miles. "Watch and learn my friends."

I rolled my eyes. Clearly, Shed favoured a very long run-up.

Shed charged towards the ball and unleashed a humungous shot. I lunged to my right as the ball went flying over the bar and landed about thirty metres behind the goal.

Brian and Dexter cracked up laughing. "We were watching but we didn't learn much!"

I tried not to chuckle too much at Shed's expression.

"I'll go and get it, shall I?" I ran towards the ball, when suddenly my caliper started making a funny noise. What was that?

I stopped for a moment and then took another step.

**CLUNK!**

I took another step.

**PING!**

I looked down just in time to see a screw roll down from inside my trouser leg and land on the grass. I frowned and stared at the small shiny object, but before I'd had time to work out fully what was happening ...

**SNAP!**

"Oh no!"

The boys came running over. "What's the matter?" asked Shed.

"I think my caliper's broken," I said. "The rod's snapped."

I tried to put pressure on my left leg, but the mechanism gave way and I crumpled to the ground.

I lay on the floor, my heartbeat pounding in my ears. Without the caliper, I can't walk.

How was I going to get home? The bikes were at the other end of the field.

Even worse, though, was this thought. What are the boys going to think, when they realise I can't walk at all? Or play football? What will they think once they realise I don't really have super-strength and I'm just a useless boy who can't even stand on his own leg?

I could feel the tears starting to build as I imagined them walking away and leaving me there, helpless. Surely they wouldn't want to be friends with me now?

That's when I felt something under my arms.

"Don't worry, we've got you," said Brian.

I felt myself being lifted up off the ground. When I looked to my side I saw that I had my arms around Brian and Dexter's shoulders. They had helped me up.

"Come on, get on," Shed said.

He'd knelt down ready for me to get on his back. Amazing.

Shed gave me a piggyback all the way to the bikes.

We didn't say much on the ride home, which thankfully didn't include another meeting with King. When we got to my house, the other three all helped me to the doorstep. I sat down and looked at my friends.

"Thanks," I said.

"Hey, we're the Parsons Road Gang," said Brian. "We stick together through thick and thin."

"Yeah," Shed said. He took a step back and, in dramatic American TV presenter style, said, "Ade is the Bionic Man! We can rebuild him!"

Even I smiled a little at that one.

"See you, Ade," said Brian. "You made some great saves today."

"Yeah, see you, Cyborg Cat," said Dexter.

I held up a hand. "See you."

But now I had to go and face the music –
Mum and Dad were not going to be pleased
with me.

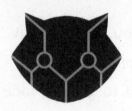

# 9
# Mr Towers

**"TUT,** tut, tut."

Mr Towers pursed his lips as he scratched the bald patch neatly sandwiched between two tufts of hair on his head. He sounded like a very old car backfiring and, even though I knew I shouldn't laugh I was struggling not to giggle.

Mr Towers is the head technician at Great Ormond Street Hospital. He was peering at me from beneath eyebrows that were extremely bushy. He was smartly dressed in a suit and bow tie, with a white lab coat on top. I knew Mr Towers was in charge of making all the appliances used by disabled children, but somehow he looked like Mr Potato Head. Thinking this didn't help with the giggles.

I looked over at Mum and Dad to see if they were laughing. They were not. They looked really worried and suddenly, my giggles evaporated.

"You've well and truly broken it," Mr Towers said, picking up the pieces of my caliper.

"Can you fix it, though?" Dad asked. "My son's due to start at school in two weeks' time. Without his caliper that's not going to happen."

Mr Towers rubbed his chin. "I'm afraid it's not straightforward."

Dad pinched the bridge of his nose and Mum bit her lip. They'd spent a long time

trying to convince Credon Primary School
to take me on as a pupil. Apparently, all the
schools in East London were worried that I
wouldn't be able to cope with the stairs. I
couldn't really understand why they thought
that. Playing football with the Parsons Road
Gang had made me super fit, but if the
school were worried it made me feel worried.

Mr Towers held the broken caliper above
his head, looking it up and down carefully.
"The thing is, this screw is easily replaced,"
he said. "But this part here has completely
snapped." Mr Towers pointed to the L-shaped
part of the caliper that slotted into the boot.

Mum and Dad looked at each other. That
really didn't sound like good news.

"But, erm, can you fix it, Mr Towers?" Mum
repeated. They were desperate to know the
answer. So was I.

"Oh, yes, of course it can be fixed,"
replied Mr Towers. "Everything can be fixed."

I felt a flash of excitement. It quickly turned to disappointment, though. Of course I wanted my caliper back, I'd really missed playing football these last few days with my mates, but I didn't really want to start school. Sure, my friends will be there, but what will everyone else be like?

Mum and Dad were looking much happier, though. I could almost see the worry leaving their bodies, like air from a balloon.

"Yes," Mr Towers said. "We'll have it as good as new for you in about six weeks."

"Six weeks!" Dad exclaimed. "But what about school?"

"It's gonna be all right, Dad," I said, secretly pleased. "It doesn't matter if I start school a few weeks late. You and Mum can teach me at home."

It was the perfect solution. I'd just decided that actually, I didn't want to go to school at all. What if the other kids were like Deano and Sam or, even worse, the horrible men in Queen's Market? I imagined arriving in the school playground with hundreds of kids staring at me and laughing at the way I walked. I could practically hear all the children whispering and giggling and then, as more and more joined in, they'd all start shouting and pointing: "Go back to your own country, Peg Leg! Nobody wants you here; go home!"

I began to shake.

"Ade? Ade? Are you okay?"

I blinked and came back to the room. Mr Towers, Mum and Dad were all staring at me as I wiped the sweat from my forehead. "Oh yeah, yeah, I'm okay."

Mr Towers frowned and turned to my parents. "Look, I can see how upset your son is about this," he said to them. "I can't promise anything, Mr and Mrs Adepitan, but I'll have a word with a few people and see if we can speed things up a little. With any luck, we may be able to get the repair time down to three weeks."

Oh great. Somehow, I'd managed to make things worse. I'd be starting school sooner rather than later after all.

Mum was beaming and Dad looked like he wanted to hug Mr Towers.

Luckily, Mr Towers distracted him. "Oh, and one more thing. To save you having to carry Ade around while we fix his caliper, I've arranged for him to have a wheelchair. You can pick it up on your way out."

No way! I hate wheelchairs. I hate the whole idea of using one. Wheelchairs are for really disabled people who can't even play football. Now I'm going to be one of them.

This was the worst day ever.

# 10
# In a bit of a fix

**BRIAN** paced up and down in my bedroom, rubbing his chin and thinking. It must have been something he'd seen on television and he was probably doing it because he thought it made him seem even more intelligent. But why would walking back and forth give you cleverer thoughts than if you were just sitting down?

Brian wasn't the only one thinking, though. Shed was on the end of my bed, bouncing a rubber ball off the floor and onto

the wall as he pondered the problem, and
Dexter was trying to balance on his head
with his legs up against the bedroom door.
He claimed it really did help him think better
and apparently it was something he always
did when the gang had a big problem to
solve.

And boy, did we have a big problem to
solve! A big, buggy-shaped problem.

"Why do you have to go in a buggy
anyway?" Dexter asked, still upside down.
"Why won't your parents let you use the
wheelchair?"

I sighed. I wanted to explain but I wasn't
sure Dex would get it. Life was really hard
for disabled people in Nigeria. There were
very few opportunities for them and, for
the most part, you only ever saw them
begging in the streets. My parents had come
to the UK because they wanted me to be
independent, to have the best life possible.

They hadn't come here to see me in a wheelchair. Dad had put his foot down. No wheelchair. He didn't want me to rely on one. To him, using a wheelchair would make his son look like he was properly disabled and he didn't agree with that.

Anyway, Mum and Dad were right. Walking is best.

"They just don't like it," I said to Dexter. "But they need to get me around somehow while my caliper is out of action."

Dexter was going red in the face so he flopped down on the floor. "Well, mate, being pushed around in a buggy is doing nothing for your reputation. A wheelchair would be so much better."

Brian glared at him. Dexter shrugged. "I'm just saying."

I lay back on the bed. Deep down, I suspected he was right. It was not a good look. "I need my caliper back, and fast."

"Definitely," Brian said. "School's starting soon."

I shook my head. "I don't care about that. I don't want to go to school; it's going to be horrible."

"No, it won't be," Shed promised. "Remember, we're the Parsons Road Gang and we always stick together." He threw the ball against the wall again, but this time it ricocheted past Shed's outstretched hand and hit Brian on the side of his head.

All the boys started laughing, apart from Brian who was anxiously examining his specs. "You could have broken my glasses. You know I can't see a thing without them."

"Chill out, Brian, it was an accident," I said. "Nothing's broken and nothing needs to be fixed."

"Hang on. That's it!" Brian shouted. "I've got it!"

"Yes, we know you've got it. The worse

case of flatulence known to man," I replied.

The boys cracked up laughing again. Brian's farts were legendary. One of his favourite meals was eggs and beans with loads of ketchup. He claimed the protein in the eggs helped him to think clearly. The problem was, they also gave him horrible wind.

"No, you sausages!" Brian spoke fast, something he did when he was about to come up with a clever idea. "Shed, your cousin Abdul is a mechanic, right?"

Shed looked confused, but nodded. "Sort of," he said. "He welds cars back together after they've been in accidents. He fixed my bike really well last summer. Made it better, actually."

Dexter jumped to his feet. "Abdul could fix Ade's caliper!"

"Correct," said Brian. "I am a genius. And yes, correct again, Abdul is the answer to our problem."

Dexter and Brian jumped in the air and chest-bumped each other in celebration. Then they did the Parsons Road Gang special handshake, which involved linking thumbs and wiggling all the other fingers.

"Hang on," I said. "Mr Towers has my caliper. There's no way he's going to give it to us to fix."

Everyone's faces fell and Brian began to pace again. He was pacing for a while, ages in fact, and then he stopped. "Well, they say the pen is mightier than the sword."

"Who says that?" Dexter looked confused.

Brian frowned. "The 'who' doesn't matter."

"What you're saying is that we should write Mr Towers a letter, right?" I said.

Brian nodded. "We'll write him a letter and say that Abdul can fix the caliper." Brian spread his arms wide. "He'll thank us. We're essentially taking work off his hands."

Shed grinned. "Great, and then we can all

start school together."

I really wanted my caliper back but the idea of starting school still filled me with fear.

"Come on," Brian said. He obviously wasn't going to take no for an answer. "Let's write this letter." He ripped the top sheet from a nearby pad of paper and handed it to me. "You should write it. It will mean more coming from you."

I knew they were right. So I nodded and began to write:

Der Mr Towers. I wood reely like it if you cud send bak my clipper so Abdul can ficks it.
Tank you veery mush.
Ade

Brian read it over my shoulder. "Well, it's definitely a unique letter. Now it just needs to be post–"

"Boys, time for you to go," Mum called up. "Your parents will be wondering where you are."

"Don't worry," I said. "Leave it to me. I know where the stamps and envelopes are kept and my mum's address book."

We did the secret handshake.

"Let me know if you need me, Ade," Shed said. "We can take it to the postbox together."

"Will do."

After dinner, I found the stamps, licked the back of one and stuck it on the envelope. It's actually pretty gross, when you think about it. It's like licking the back of the Queen's head or something. I don't think she'd like that very much if anyone did it for real.

Now there was only one thing left to do. Post the letter.

"Mum," I shouted. "Can I go round to

Shed's? I need to show him something."

"Yes," Mum said. "But only a quick visit. It's bedtime soon. Do you want me to take you in the buggy?"

"NO!" That would be awful. "It's not far. I can get there."

A few minutes later, I was at Shed's doorstep, dripping with sweat.

"What happened to you?" Shed asked, looking at the state of me.

"I hopped all the way round."

"You should have just called me, you doughnut." Shed shook his head.

"Come on, let's go post this letter." I held the envelope aloft, brandishing it like it was the FA Cup.

The nearest postbox was five streets away and by the time we got there, Shed was the one who was sweating. He'd given me a piggyback all the way.

"This is going to work," I said, holding the

letter up again. "I believe in the power of the Parsons Road Gang."

"Yeah," gasped Shed, out of breath. "The ... power ... of the ... Parsons Road Gang ... can make anything happen."

"Here goes." I slid the precious letter into the opening of the postbox and held it there for a couple of seconds before letting it go.

Ten minutes later we were back outside my house.

"Thanks, Shed," I said as he knelt down to let me off his back.

Shed slumped to the ground next to me, exhausted, and just about managed to mumble, "No problem."

"Hey, what's up with you two?"

We looked up. It was Brian. "Shed just took me to post the letter," I told him.

"Right," said Brian, looking at Shed who was breathing heavily and gradually slumped even further down. "But why did Shed have to take you? Why didn't you just ask him to go and post the letter for you?"

I looked at Shed and he looked at me. Then we both burst out laughing, realising at the exact same moment how silly we'd been.

When we'd calmed down, I looked at Brian and Shed and said, "I believe in the power of the Parsons Road Gang."

"Yeah," said Shed. "It's so strong, I'll bet we'll get your caliper back and fixed by tomorrow."

# 11
# No time to lose

**MY** caliper did not arrive for Abdul to fix the next day.

Or the one after.

Or the one after that.

By the middle of the following week, I was feeling truly miserable. Mum had taken me out in the buggy three more times. Some people just stared, but others would come up and pat me on the head and say how cute I looked. Cute! One woman had even taken a rattle out of her bag and given it to me.

Even worse was when a group of kids had started laughing and making baby noises.

I told Mum and Dad how much I hated the buggy and I begged them not to make me use it. "Can't I just stay at home until my caliper is fixed?"

But Dad was having none of it. "Come on. You're not hiding in this house."

School was due to start in five days' time and the other boys were all getting ready. They'd done their best to keep my spirits up, but nothing much was working. I still didn't want to go to school at all, but if I had to go, what I really, *really* didn't want was to start weeks later than everyone else. I didn't want to turn up when everyone else had settled in. I was going to stick out like a sore thumb anyway, but arriving on my own would make it a hundred times worse.

By the time Friday came around I was wishing I could just fall asleep and wake up back in Nigeria. Maybe the whole thing was just a bad dream. Lying on my bed, I imagined playing with my cousins at Gran Gran's house, running around, looking out for colobus monkeys leaping acrobatically through the trees ...

"Doyin! Doyin! Come quickly! Doyin!"

I pushed myself off the bed and shuffled downstairs. Mum was running around, putting her coat on and looking for the house keys.

"Mum, what is it? Is everything okay?"

"The hospital called, Doyin. They said your caliper is ready. If we can get there by five, they can fit it today."

"It's fixed?" I said. "But Abdul didn't –"

"Abdul?" repeated Mum. She shook her head. "Doyin, it's almost four, we've got to hurry if they're going to fit it today. Get ready."

Five minutes later, I was in the buggy and being pushed to the bus stop on Barking

Road as fast as Mum could go.

As we got to the bus stop I heard someone snort with laughter. I closed my eyes. Why did Mum put me in this stupid buggy?

"Interesting choice of socks," a girl's voice said.

"Huh?" I opened my eyes. She didn't sound unfriendly. A tall girl with springy hair and golden-brown skin was leaning against the bus stop. Her hands were in her tracksuit pockets.

She barely glanced at the buggy; it was like she hadn't seen it. "If you're gonna wear superhero socks, I would go for Iceman; Wolverine is way too obvious."

Still confused, I looked down at my bright yellow-and-black socks. My knees were up by my chin as I sat hunched uncomfortably in the baby buggy so my socks were on show. Wolverine scowled angrily from my feet as if he agreed with the strange girl.

"Yup, definitely the wrong choice," she said.

Definitely the wrong choice. My heart skipped a beat as her words reminded me of something. I suddenly realised what it was.

"Wait!" I shouted.

"What, Doyin? What is it?" Mum cried. "What's wrong?"

"I should be in the wheelchair, Mum! Mr Towers gave it to us. What will he think when he sees me in a buggy?"

"Oh, Lord, Doyin, you're right."

My head flew back as Mum tilted the buggy onto its rear wheels and spun it round. As we shot off back home I heard the girl at the bus stop say, "See you later, Wolverine."

She was grinning, her large eyes twinkling with humour.

I wasn't sure how to respond, but it was too late anyway as Mum sprinted back down

Parsons Road. We swapped the buggy for the wheelchair and, now even later than we'd been before, charged back to the bus stop.

As we waited for the number 5 to arrive, Mum went really quiet. I could tell she was nervous, and not just about us being late. She was probably worried about getting the wheelchair on the bus.

In Nigeria the buses were usually old and battered, and crammed full of more people than a tin of sardines who had invited all their fishy friends over to stay. People in wheelchairs didn't ride the buses much. If anyone in a wheelchair did ever try to get on, the chair would be strapped to the roof and the person shoved in with everyone else, packed in tight. On top of that, the drivers drove like maniacs, as if they were Formula One racing drivers in a real hurry.

"Don't worry, Mum," I said. "It'll be okay."

Mum nodded and stroked my cheek. I liked it, but I was kind of glad the girl had gone.

When the bus finally arrived we both breathed a huge sigh of relief. It was fairly empty and there was plenty of room for the wheelchair. A couple of the other passengers even moved seats to make things easier.

I spent the whole journey willing cars to get out of the way and telepathically trying to tell the driver to speed up. Mum obviously felt the same: I think she would have liked them to be a bit more Nigerian and actually drive like the bus was in a Formula One race.

Whether our silent wishes for it to hurry up worked or not was difficult to know, but we reached the stop at ten to five, got off the bus and raced to Great Ormond Street Hospital.

Mum burst through the main entrance pushing me and headed straight to the lifts. But ...

"Oh no," said Mum. "They're out of order. How am I going to get you up to Mr Towers' office on the third floor?"

It looked as if we'd come all that way in vain. It was almost five o'clock. I wasn't going to be able to start school on Monday, after all.

"Can we help?"

Mum and I turned to see where the voice had come from and saw two nurses.

"Oh, erm, yes," said Mum. "We need to get to the third floor and the lift is broken."

The nurses looked at each other. "Come on, young man, up you get."

Couldn't they see the wheelchair? I was just about to say that I obviously couldn't get up when I felt myself being lifted up and onto the nurse's shoulders, while the other one folded up the wheelchair and carried it up the stairs.

My nostrils started to flare; they always

do that when I'm angry or frustrated. I didn't want their help. I didn't ask for their help. I need to get fitter and stronger, so I can do things by myself. But I knew from the look on Mum's face I needed to keep quiet.

"Thank you," Mum said.

The nurse shrugged. "We're just sorry the lifts are broken."

At two minutes to five we were outside Mr Towers' office.

"Ah, you made it," said Mr Towers as we went inside. "Good to see you again. Now then, take a look at this." Mr Towers opened a box and pulled out my caliper. "Good as new, eh?"

I couldn't believe my eyes. It really did look as good as new. Once Mr Towers had fitted it, it turned out the caliper was even better than new. Mr Towers had created a hinge with a lever that allowed me to bend my leg at the knee when I was wearing it.

It was amazing; I hadn't been able to do that before.

"Thank you so much, Mr Towers," said Mum. "But tell me, how were you able to fix it so quickly?"

"Well," said Mr Towers, looking at me. "I received a letter. And, let's just say, reading it made me think that perhaps it would be a good idea for Ade to start school as soon as possible and, when he does, to work very, very hard at his spelling."

# 12
# Pretty in Pink

**"WAKE** up, Doyin. Wake up!"

I opened my eyes.

"It's seven thirty," Mum said. "Time to get up for school."

I stared at Mum, bleary-eyed.

"Are you okay?" Mum looked concerned. "You were talking in your sleep. You kept on saying, 'No, please no.'"

"Yeah, I'm okay. I just had a bad dream," I said. "But I can't quite remember it."

Mum gave me a big hug. "Don't worry,

everybody gets nervous on their first day at a new school." She put her hand on my head. "You wait and see, by the end of the afternoon you'll be having such a good time you probably won't want to come home."

Yeah, right. But Mum's warm smile and her reassuring voice did make me feel a little better.

"Now, hurry up and get dressed," she said. "Your new suit is all ready for you."

Oh no!

The suit.

*That* was what I'd been dreaming about. In that moment, everything about our trip back to Queen's Market the day before came flooding back in a rush.

I hadn't wanted to go in the first place. What if we saw those horrible men again? But Mum had said I needed a new outfit for school and there's no arguing with Mum.

What had happened was bad enough to give me nightmares.

As soon as we had left the house, I could feel myself getting anxious. As we approached the actual market, my heart began pounding so hard it felt as if I had a full-on orchestra in my chest. I felt hot and sweaty, and I was glad I could walk and wasn't being pushed around. I gripped Mum's hand tightly.

Soon, the familiar sounds of market traders selling their goods started to fill the air. After what had happened the last time we'd been there, I was surprised at how calm Mum seemed. She talked and joked with people on the stalls as we wandered round.

I relaxed my shoulders a bit, and my grip on Mum's hand. The market felt like a very different place this time, much friendlier, a place where people came to have a good time, not to be shouted at by thugs.

I dragged Mum over to a toy stall. If I played my cards right, I reckoned I could get her to buy me something. I was playing with a Darth Vader figure when a deep voice made me jump.

"Back again, then?"

A chill ran down the back of my neck. I turned around. Standing in front of the stall opposite was a man with a face I recognised, but to my relief it wasn't an ugly, snarling one. It was a very round, red, cheery face, and when the man smiled it seemed to double in size and his funny checked hat almost popped off his head.

I remembered him. It was the trader who'd looked like he'd wanted to take on the horrible men when they'd started threatening my parents.

"Hello. I'm Glenn Warrick." He extended a massive hand in greeting to Mum. His huge chubby fingers looked just like sausages.

King would love those!

"Just so you know," Glenn went on. "We ain't all like those idiots who were shouting at you that time." His cheeks got even redder. "Sorry you had to go through that. Some people are just wrong 'uns!"

For a moment there was silence. Then Mum stretched out her hand to shake his. "Pleased to meet you, Glenn."

She gave me a gentle nudge forwards.

"Pleased to meet you, too," I said. My hand disappeared inside Glenn's grip and I wondered if I'd ever see it again.

"Right, madam, can I interest you in anything in particular?" Glenn pointed proudly at his stall, which was heaving with a vast array of trousers, blazers, jumpers and suits, all neatly laid out or dangling from hangers.

Mum cast her wily shopper's gaze over his goods.

"I'll tell you what I'll do," Glenn said. "You can have a special discount on anything you like today. Twenty per cent off just for you, Mrs ...?"

"Mrs Adepitan," she said.

"Righto," said Glenn. "And who might you be, young fella?"

"I'm Ade," I said. "My name is Ah-dee. Not Eddie, not Adrian, and definitely not Ade, like at the end of lemonade."

"Oh, he's sharp, isn't he?" Glenn said. "You got a right one there, love."

But Mum wasn't listening. Her eye had been drawn to something on the stall.

"How about that one?" she said, pointing. "How much would that be?"

I followed Mum's finger to where she was pointing. Oh no.

There, blazing out amongst the nice, normal black, grey and dark blue suits, was the brightest pink checked blazer with matching flared trousers that I, or indeed anyone, had ever seen.

"Well, well, well, Mrs Apepijan!" said Glenn.

"ADEPITAN," she corrected him.

"Pardon me, madam," said the stallholder. "Now then, you certainly know your fashion, don't you? This is a lovely number. Hundred per cent wool, guaranteed not to shrink."

As Glenn started to go into his sales patter, I felt my heart sink. No, surely not! Mum can't possibly be thinking about buying that suit for me. It's louder and brighter than the Big Bang.

"Oh yeah," Glenn continued. "You're definitely gonna make an impression in this suit. No one's gonna miss you, young man, that's for sure. It's a great colour. What's the occasion? Party? Wedding? Carnival?"

"Oh no," said Mum. "It's for Ade to wear tomorrow; it's his first day of school."

Glenn paused. He gulped. He looked at me with pity.

"First day of school?" he said. "Well, it's very nice and that, but don't you think it'd be better for him to try something a little less, erm, colourful?"

Thank goodness! I nodded furiously, wide-eyed. "Yes, Mum."

Glenn pointed at a very plain black suit. "That one might be –"

"Oh no." Mum cut him off. "This is most definitely the one. It's beautiful." Then, to confirm her belief, she picked up the blazer and added, "Yes and very good quality material, as well."

Glenn looked at me and shrugged, as if to say, *Sorry, mate. A sale is a sale.*

That's it, I'm done for. I knew there was no escape. Mum was going to buy me not only the worst suit in London, not even the worst suit in the UK, but also the worst suit in the *entire world*.

Not even the Parsons Road Gang would want to hang out with the boy with the funny walk and the pink, checked, flared suit.

I was going to be a giant, limping stick of candyfloss.

"Go on, Doyin, get your suit. Let's see how you look."

I blinked hard. I was back in my room, memories of yesterday swiftly fading, and Mum was sitting on the edge of the bed.

Slowly, I dragged myself out of bed and went over to the cupboard. "Please have changed colour in the night," I whispered to myself.

I opened the door. The suit hadn't changed colour. If anything it beamed out at me even more brightly than yesterday. Full-on pinky checked-ness.

I gritted my teeth. Okay, the suit wasn't going anywhere. It was time to get this over and done with.

Suddenly, out of nowhere, I felt some laughter bubbling up. If you don't laugh, you'll cry.

I just hoped I'd still be laughing at the end of the day.

# 13
# Fashion Show!

**"SO** handsome!" said Mum as I headed towards the front door.

I almost couldn't bear to look in the hallway mirror. To complete my 'look', Mum had insisted on combing my hair into a massive Afro, which made my head look like a giant microphone. And, to finish things off, she'd made me wear a large, black velvet bow tie! There was no arguing with her.

I looked ridiculous.

They were so proud of me, though. Their

son. Their son who had polio as a baby and wears a caliper on his leg is going to a regular school like all the other kids. It hadn't been easy for Mum and Dad, I knew that.

Mrs Bolton, the headteacher at Credon Road Primary, had expressed serious reservations. The school was nearly a hundred years old, parts of it had been bombed during the Second World War and the building had been reconstructed on three floors. Getting around involved climbing up and down stairs, lots of stairs. I knew that I was going to be the first disabled child of any kind to attend the school. And it was happening because my parents had dreamed and fought so hard for this moment.

So they were full of pride and I was just full of fear. Fear about what people would laugh at first: my leg, my dodgy pink suit or my crazy hair. Perhaps they'll end up so confused they'll just leave me alone. Hmm.

As I stepped out of the front door I was beginning to think that my mother wasn't completely deluded. Maybe she was actually a genius. What if she had made her son look as geeky as possible on purpose? What if she'd done it so the bullies wouldn't know where to start with me?

I shook my head in frustration. No, that was crazy. It was more likely that the bullies would all queue up to get me on my first day. I turned and looked back at Mum and Dad, who were standing together by the front door and waving.

"Remember," Mum called. "No football with your new caliper."

I nodded and managed to make it to the garden gate without anyone on the street giving me any grief, which, under the circumstances, was quite an achievement. I'd have laughed if I'd been a passer-by and seen me dressed like this. I smiled weakly back at Mum and Dad and walked on.

Dexter, Brian and Shed had all come out of their houses at the same time. As they reached their front gates, they all looked at me standing on the pavement.

Dexter was the first to speak. "All right, Ade," he said in an unusually shy voice.

Dexter was wearing a bright red jumper and a pair of black trousers with red pinstripes running down them. Over that he had a huge parka coat that was about two sizes too big for him.

I tried not to laugh.

"What!?" Dexter shouted defiantly. "It's my brother's coat. I'll grow into it! Anyway, what are you wearing, MISTER PINK SUIT?"

Dexter said the last bit in a posh, high-pitched voice, which made me start giggling. Dexter joined in.

"Oi, what are you two laughing at?" said

Brian, standing in his gateway. He was wearing a pair of brown corduroy trousers and a yellow tank top over a white shirt, a combination that only made us laugh even harder. Brian couldn't see the funny side. He thought he looked smart. He'd picked out the tank top personally.

Finally, we all turned and looked at Shed as he walked towards us. He was wearing an ill-fitting pair of lime green jeans. They were at least two sizes too small for him and made him look like a young version of the Incredible Hulk. He also had on a smart shirt with his sleeves rolled up to the elbow. The four of us really were quite a sight, a sort of weird rainbow of strange-fitting clothes, and soon the whole Parsons Road Gang were falling about laughing.

"Seriously, I think we all look cool," Brian said, trying his best to keep a straight face.

"Looks like your mums have all been

getting fashion tips from mine," I said.

Suddenly, a shrill voice came from the upstairs window of Dexter's house. "Oi, Dexter, stop jabbering and get to school. If you don't hurry up you'll be late."

It was Dexter's mum. She still had curlers in her hair and her face was bright red. This would usually have made us laugh even more, but she sounded quite cross, so we all tried hard to look as serious as possible and started walking to school. Once we were out of sight, and sure Dexter's mum couldn't hear us, we all cracked up and started making fun of each other's clothes again.

Maybe the other kids at school would see the funny side of it as well and we'd all end up having a big laugh about it.

Maybe.

# 14
# Playground Panic

I leant back and craned my neck. Credon Road Primary School was three storeys high. Huge arched windows lined up in rows on each floor; in combination with the dark brown bricks that surrounded them, the school looked quite sinister against the grey cloudy sky.

Apart from the hospital, this was going to be the tallest building I'd ever been in and, unlike the hospital, I knew there were no lifts if I needed them. Okay, the one at the hospital had been broken, but still. Looking up at the top row of windows, I imagined climbing all those stairs myself and gulped.

Turning my attention back to ground level, I looked at my friends. They all seemed as nervous as I was, but I guessed it wasn't the building they were concerned about.

Walking into the playground, we were confronted by a teeming mass of children running, skipping, chasing, jumping and, in some cases, just standing around chatting. The noise was incredible; you could probably hear it from at least two streets away.

"I'd forgotten how big this place was," Dexter said.

"And noisy," Brian added. "I can hardly hear myself think."

"It's not Southern Road Playing Fields, that's for sure." Shed sounded wistful.

This whole time I was worrying about going to school, I hadn't really thought about how the rest of them were feeling. We'd had the best summer together and now it was all going to change. It had been just the four of us and now there were hundreds of kids to deal with.

"Hey," I said as cheerily as possible.

"What?" they all replied.

"Never forget, we're the Parsons Road Gang!"

Brian smiled. Dexter nodded, and Shed looked at us and said, "Yeah, and we always stick together!"

"Yeah!" shouted the other three, punching the air.

## DOOFF!

A leather football hit Brian square on the nose. My friend's blue-rimmed glasses flew off his face.

Brian wiped his nose, realised there was no blood then dropped to his knees and instantly began scrabbling around on the playground trying to find his glasses. Shed and Dexter helped.

I spotted Brian's glasses next to a water fountain and picked them up, but saw straight away that the left lens had shattered, creating a pattern that looked like a spider's web in the glass.

"You all right, Brian?" I asked, passing them back to my friend. "Afraid these are a bit broken."

"My mum's going to kill me," said Brian, gingerly putting them back on. "But at least they're not completely broken, even if it does feel like I'm looking out of a kaleidoscope."

"Oi! Give our ball back, you freaks!" said an unpleasant-sounding voice.

Standing there with three other kids was a short, extremely stocky boy with dark curly hair, pale skin and round, puffy cheeks.

"Oh no!" muttered Dexter. "Spencer Frogley."

"We don't know where your ball is," Shed said. Even though Shed was pretty big, his voice sounded rather small.

"But when you find it, be careful where you kick it from now on," I said. "You broke Brian's glasses."

As I spoke, I noticed that Spencer's eyes seemed to bulge out of his head and double in size, making him actually look like a frog. A frog with curly hair.

"Are you telling me what to do?" Spencer looked round at his cronies like he couldn't quite believe it. "Look at the state of you all."

"What a bunch of muppets," said one of Spencer's friends. "They must have escaped from the circus."

As they laughed, I could feel every child in the playground staring at me and my friends. My stomach began to churn. It was the same sort of feeling I'd had in Queen's Market the first time I'd been there. And when I'd seen Deano and Sam outside my house on the day of the party. It was a sort of mixture of anger and fear.

I looked at my friends to see their reactions.

Shed was looking down intently at something on the ground, while Brian was busy trying to adjust his broken glasses.

"I think the frame is twisted," he muttered anxiously under his breath.

Even Dexter was unusually quiet.

"Come on, freaks, the ball's right next to you," shouted Spencer. "Don't you know how to use your arms? Chuck the ball back!"

I glared at Spencer and then, without thinking, picked up the football and with an almighty heave of my right arm I threw it as hard as I could towards the other boys, who were still laughing amongst themselves. I could feel my caliper giving me a weird sort of power, as if it was connected to something, giving me courage and strength.

The ball sailed over their heads and through the goal Spencer and his friends had made using their coats.

*"GOOOAAAL!"* I screamed, in the style of a Brazilian commentator.

Shed suddenly looked up and beamed at me.

"Yeah, the Cyborg Cat does it again!" shouted Dexter, springing to life and laughing hysterically.

"Take it easy, guys," Brian hissed. He glanced in the direction of Spencer and his mates. "They're coming over."

"You think that was funny?" Spencer said angrily, practically face-to-face with me.

"If you mean the fact that I managed to throw a football into your goal without hitting your huge head then, yes," I replied with a smirk.

Spencer Frogley didn't scare me. I was the Cyborg Cat, after all.

Spencer's friends started to giggle, but stopped suddenly when he turned and glared at them.

"Look, gentlemen, there seems to have been a slight misunderstanding," Brian started to say, using what he called his calming voice; the one he used whenever we needed something from grown-ups. "Why don't we all – "

"Shut it, Four Eyes," Spencer growled.

He turned back to me.

We glared at each other.

It. Was. On.

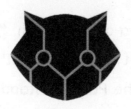

# 15
# Play that melody

I was not going to blink first. I knew it for a fact, because I was really, really good at this game. I used to play it with my cousins at Gran Gran's house.

"Erm, I've got an idea," Dexter said, breaking the tension. "And it doesn't involve eyeballing each other."

One of Spencer's mates lunged towards him, but Spencer blocked him with an arm. "Let's hear what the idiot in the red jumper's got to say."

Dexter took a deep breath. "Why don't we sort this out with a football match? Your team against the Parsons Road Gang."

I was trying to get Dexter's attention but he wasn't looking at me.

Spencer started laughing again. "The what gang?" he said.

Spencer's friends all broke into fits of laughter, and so did a large group of children who had gathered round to see what was going on.

"You bunch of freaks don't stand a chance!" Spencer said, high-fiving his friends. "We're the best players in this school."

One of his mates was skinny with blond hair and freckles. The other boy was dark-haired with huge, powerful legs that looked like tree trunks.

"Stuart and John go to West Ham's junior academy," Spencer said with a swagger. "We'd run rings round you."

"So, you're saying you won't take us on?" said Dexter.

"What do you think, lads?" said Spencer to John and Stuart.

The academy stars shrugged. "Yeah, why not?" said John. "It'll kill time before school starts."

"Right," said Spencer, pointing to the goal I'd just thrown the ball through. "See you for your total annihilation. Over there, two minutes."

Spencer and his friends walked off to prepare for the match.

My shoulders drooped and I breathed for what felt like the first time in ages. Then I turned to Dexter.

"You idiot."

"What you worried about, Ade?" Dexter said, putting a calming hand on my shoulder. "This will be easy."

"Yeah, we can take them," agreed Shed.

"We've been practising all summer; we're more than ready for this challenge."

I looked at the boys and shook my head. "Haven't you all forgotten something?" The boys looked back at me, bemused.

"What?" they said as one.

"No more football. I can't play, remember? My mum said I'm not supposed to in case my caliper breaks again!"

My words hit the boys like a ton of bricks. Dexter went pale, Shed swallowed hard and said in shock, "No Cyborg Cat?" Brian let out a huge sigh and started to fiddle nervously with his smashed glasses. "If we're down to three men we don't stand a chance," he said.

"What's the matter, you freaks, chickening out?" Spencer jeered.

"Th... there see...see... seems to be a slight problem," Brian stuttered. "A crucial member of our team," Brian paused and nodded in my direction, "can't play because his Mu... erm ... because he's injured."

Spencer focused his bulgy eyes on me again. "You mean he can't play because he's a stupid peg-leg cripple!"

More laughter broke out. There were some gasps and squeals; some of the children nearby had obviously noticed my leg and, in particular, the hospital boots and the iron rods coming out of the heel. I felt sick. It felt like the whole school was staring at me. I hate being called a cripple.

"Look," said Dexter amidst the commotion. "How about we make it three against three?"

"No way," spat Spencer. "You challenged us to this match; if you haven't got enough players on your side that's not our problem."

"But that's not fair!" shouted Shed.

"Yeah," chipped in Brian. "And I can only see out of one eye 'cause you broke my glasses."

"Shouldn't have got your stupid big nose

in the way of the ball then, should you?" retorted Spencer. "Now, we gonna start or what?"

It looked like we were going to lose whatever happened. But then ...

"I'll play on their team."

The voice came from somewhere amongst the kids who had gathered around the two rival groups.

A tall girl with springy black hair had forced her way to the front of the crowd. She looked familiar. Then I recognized her. It was the girl from the bus stop!

She walked over to me.

"I'm Melody Roberts," she said. "I'm in the same year as you."

We looked at each other, then back at Melody. We all just stood there in silence and stared at her, open-mouthed. We seemed unable to speak.

Melody shook her head, clearly

unimpressed, and said, "Are you boys gonna stand there like total idiots or are we going to beat those other idiots over there?"

The gang continued to look at each other. I knew what was befuddling their brains because it was befuddling my brain, too.

"She's a girl," Shed eventually blurted out.

"She's a girl," Melody responded, mimicking Shed's voice. "Wow, we've got a smart one here. Yes, I'm a girl. And?"

"This is just perfect," yelled Spencer. "They've swapped the cripple for a girl!"

Melody glowered fiercely in Spencer's direction then grabbed the football and started doing keepy-uppies.

When she got to twenty, my brain clicked back into gear. I'd suddenly realised two things. One, we had to win this game or we'd end up being the butt of the whole school's jokes for the rest of our time at Credon. And two, we *needed* Melody on our team.

"LET'S START," I shouted. "If I can't play, I'll be the manager. Brian, you go in goal; Dexter, up front with Melody."

"Hey, Melody," said Dexter. "I'm just warning you now to cover your eyes, as you're about to be dazzled by the best right foot in London."

"We'll see about that," said Melody, and the two of them raced off, passing the ball between them as they went.

"What about me, gaffer?" Shed asked, looking at me.

"Midfield, of course, Shed. Make sure nothing gets past you."

Shed pounded his chest and gave me a determined look. Moments later, it was kick-off.

# 16
# The most important match of our lives

I paced up and down on the sidelines. The first few exchanges had been fast and furious. It was clear that Stuart and John were pretty good, but Shed was doing his job in midfield and, with Dexter and Melody tracking back and helping him out, the two academy trainees weren't able to break through.

Brian was also doing well in goal, despite only really being able to see out of one eye, and, after he'd saved a shot from Spencer, he spotted Melody free on the right and threw the ball out to her.

Melody trapped it and immediately set off. Her close control was fantastic! I watched her dribble round all of Spencer's team effortlessly. She approached the goal and I held my breath. She skillfully slotted the ball straight past Spencer's goalkeeper.

*"GOOOAL!"* I yelled, whooping in delight. "What an unbelievable goal!"

Melody high-fived Dexter and just laughed at Shed, who was still speechless. I think he was a bit in awe of our new star player.

"Come on." Spencer was furious. "We're not getting beaten by this bunch of weirdos!"

By now, pretty much the whole school had gathered round to watch the match.

Even the teacher on morning playground duty was watching intently from a distance.

I could see that Spencer's rage, and

the fact that they'd gone a goal down,
had seemed to energise our opponents. I
watched a slick passing move between John
and Stuart. They were getting it together.
Then, in a flash, it happened – an incisive
pass from John put Stuart through on goal.

I knew what was coming.

Stuart blasted the ball towards the left-
hand corner of the goal.

Brian looked to have it covered, but just
as he was about to dive towards the ball,
he lost his footing and hit the ground. Once
again, his glasses flew off his face.

*"YESSS!"* cheered Stuart, punching the air
with a clenched fist as the ball flew into the
goal to make the score 1–1.

"That's more like it, lads!" Spencer
screamed, his eyes bulging so much they
almost came out of their sockets. He gave
Stuart a bear hug and lifted him off the
ground in celebration.

"Looks like luck's running out for the Pampers Road Gang!" Spencer yelled, pointing at me.

I raced over to Brian, flicked the lever on my caliper and knelt down beside him. Brian was looking dazed, with his broken glasses in his hands.

"Are you okay?" I asked as Shed, Dexter and Melody came over.

Brian got to his feet, swayed on the spot and took a step towards the wall.

"I feel a bit funny," he said. "Don't think I can play any more." He held up what was left of his glasses. "These have had it."

"Er, Brian," I started to say, but before I could finish, Brian had raised his hand to interrupt.

In his best calming voice, he said, "Ade, I know your mum said you're not allowed to play football but, listen to me. We need you. The Parsons Road Gang needs you! We need the Cyborg Cat."

"I will listen to you, Brian," I said, grinning. "But first you need to turn around, because you're talking to a wall. I'm behind you."

"Ah!" Brian turned round. "I must have hit my head harder than I thought."

"Come on, Pampers Gang! We haven't got all day." Spencer's voice was loud and mocking.

I looked at Spencer. If we don't win this game, all the other kids in the school will treat me and my friends the way Spencer is treating us now. But my parents will kill me if I play football and something happens to my caliper again.

"Come on, Cripple Boy," Spencer taunted. "What are you lot doing?"

*Cripple.*

I hate that word. I *really* hate it. It was what that horrible man in Queen's Market had called me. It does not describe me.

"I'll go in goal," I said immediately.

"Yes!" Dexter exclaimed. "Get ready for Cyborg Cat."

As I took up my position I knew this could all end very badly. What if the teachers tell my parents I'd played football? Or my caliper breaks again? But I didn't really have a choice. I wasn't going to let my friends down and I needed to show everyone what I was capable of.

I was Cyborg Cat. If I believed in myself the way the Parsons Road Gang believed in me, we could win.

The game restarted. Spencer's team launched wave after wave of attack, but the Parsons Road defence held firm. When a shot did get through, I was ready. Cyborg Cat made three spectacular saves and then Shed somehow managed to get the ball off one of the other players. I smiled to myself. Spencer was getting angrier and angrier.

From the sidelines, Brian, who was holding the one good lens from his glasses to his right eye, hollered, "Through ball, Shed."

Shed was not known for his accuracy when it came to passing but, to his own surprise, and everyone else's, he coolly lofted the perfect pass straight over Spencer to Melody.

Melody controlled the ball with one touch and looked up. Dexter was up front screaming, "I'm open. Get it to my right foot!"

A moment later, Melody had crossed the ball beautifully to Dexter. As it came over he pulled his right foot back, ready to hit the ball sweetly and bury it in the back of the net, even though there was no net. It was definitely going to be one of the greatest goals ever scored in Credon Primary School playground.

Well, it would have been, had it not been

for the fact that Dexter missed the ball completely.

I groaned.

But all was not lost. The ball ricocheted off Dexter's right foot, bounced up and struck him in the face. The goalie had already flung himself towards the shot he was expecting, and Spencer and his team could only watch in horror as the ball rolled across the line from Dexter's accidental header, making it 2–1 to the Parsons Road Gang.

We all jumped in the air, screaming with delight.

"Did I score?" Dexter asked, rubbing his nose.

"Of course you did, you sausage!" Brian bellowed, and the whole team huddled together and began to jump on the spot.

"It's not over yet!" Spencer hollered. He picked up the ball.

We were still celebrating as he restarted the game. "Oi!" I yelled, seeing what he was doing a moment too late and trying to get back to goal.

"Yeah, wait a minute," shouted Dexter.

But it was no good. Spencer had passed the ball to Stuart, who took a shot at the empty goal.

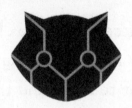

# 17
# Cyborg Cat

**SHED** launched himself through the air and made a last-ditch crunching tackle. He didn't connect with the ball, but he did connect with Stuart's legs, sending him to the ground in a painful heap.

"Penalty!" yelled Spencer. "That's got to be a penalty."

I didn't want to agree, but I nodded. Yeah, that was fair. Even though the Parson's Road Gang hadn't been ready to restart the game, I had to admit that it was a terrible tackle.

Shed ran over to Stuart, who was writhing on the ground clutching his ankle. "Sorry, mate," he said.

"No worries." Stuart jumped to his feet with a grin, instantly recovered. "We've got a penalty."

"I'm taking it." Spencer walked over to my goal. He counted out ten paces and put the ball down. "This is the penalty spot," he announced.

It seemed a bit too close to the goal to me but no one else questioned it. Spencer didn't look like he would listen anyway.

"You can do it, Ade," shouted Shed from the sidelines. "The Cyborg Cat's got this."

"Yeah," shouted the others.

## THUDDD!

Spencer hammered the ball as hard as he could towards the goal.

As it hurtled through the air, I knew I

really was Cyborg Cat. My caliper was super-powered, giving me strength. I was as fast as a cat and as strong as a cyborg. I launched myself to my right, my arm stretched out as far as it would go.

**CRACK!**

The ball hit my outstretched finger-tips. It was just enough to push it wide of the goal by a centimetre.

**DUMPH!**

I hit the concrete playground. Not even the shoulder pads in my pink suit could protect me from the painful landing.

There was silence. Then the teacher's whistle. Class was about to start. The match was over.

Dexter, Shed, Brian and Melody came running over. I sat up. I didn't think I was ready to stand.

"Yesss!" screamed Dexter. "Adepitan the

super Cyborg Cat saves the day."

"I told you we could do it," Shed shouted.

"That's 2-1 to the Parsons Road Gang!" Brian hollered.

Melody leapt in the air singing, "Champi-o-nes, champi-o-nes, ole ole ole!"

The whole playground seemed to have erupted into celebration around us.

"Nice work, new boy," one of the older kids yelled over to me. Another caught my eye and gave me a thumbs up.

Maybe school wasn't going to be too bad, after all.

John and Stuart came over to shake hands. "Good game, guys."

Spencer was nowhere to be seen, though. He'd gone off to sulk.

As the crowd dispersed and poured into school, I began to dust myself off. Pink did not look good dirty! Then I froze.

"Uh-oh."

"What's wrong?" said Shed.

I looked towards my leg. "I think I've broken it."

"No!" shouted Brian with a look of dread on his face.

I looked at the gang solemnly. Their faces were a picture.

"Yeah, I think I've broken a toenail on my left foot."

It took a moment for the gang to realise what I'd said. Then they all burst out laughing.

"You silly sausage!" Brian shouted and with that, the boys all piled on top of me and continued celebrating.

Melody stood watching us, shaking her head and smiling. "You lot are ridiculous," she said as the teacher blew the whistle again for final warning to get to class.

\* \* \*

For the rest of the school day the Parsons Road Gang and Melody were heroes. Everyone had seen the morning's events. I even heard someone call us the 'Spencer Slayers'!

Dexter suggested putting this on T-shirts and selling them. I wasn't too sure about that idea.

I had a feeling Spencer was going to be someone they needed to avoid and rubbing his face it in would definitely not be a good plan.

At the end of school, we waved goodbye to Melody as she jumped on her blue Raleigh BMX with white mag wheels.

"She's amazing!" Shed said, as she rode off. "Even her bike is super-cool."

"Yes, she's quite remarkable," said Brian. "For a girl."

"She's quite remarkable for a human being," I said. "She's got to be the best footballer I've ever seen."

Brian and Shed nodded in agreement.

Dexter shrugged. "She needs to work on her left foot."

I grinned. "She's not the only one. But seriously, she helped us out today and she's a brilliant player – shall we ask her tomorrow if she wants to be in the gang?" They all agreed it was a good idea and we walked on towards Parsons Road.

"So, still think school is going to be horrible, Ade?" Shed asked me.

"Nah, today's been great. Better than great, actually. I don't think it could get any bett..."

I trailed off because there was a strange sound. There was the rhythmic bouncing of a ball on concrete, followed by another noise, one I'd never heard before. I couldn't place it.

"What is that?" Brian said, hearing it too.

A moment later, Brian's question was answered when an LA Lakers basketball suddenly appeared out of nowhere in front of us. It bounced on the pavement and then, before it could bounce again, a long, powerful arm reached out and grabbed it.

It was quite a move. An athletic-looking boy had sped up alongside us. He wasn't running, though. He was in a bright red wheelchair with white discs in the middle of the wheels. Each disc had been painted with red, yellow and orange flames, which made it look like the wheels were on fire as they whizzed round. The unusual noise we'd heard was the wheelchair's tyres making a skidding sound as the boy used his hands to control it.

"WHOA!" we all said in unison.

"All right," said the boy in the chair as he

briskly rolled past, skilfully controlling the basketball and his wheelchair at the same time.

He didn't look much older than me and my friends, but his muscular physique and powerful arms made him look twice our size. He was wearing a basketball vest with the words 'Newham Rollers' on the front. He zoomed past us and soon became a dot in the distance.

"Who was that?" I was desperate to find out.

Shed shook his head. "I don't know, but I think that was the coolest thing I've ever seen."

"Yeah, I suppose so," I muttered.

For some reason I felt a bit weird. I'd always thought using a wheelchair meant that a person was helpless. But that boy wasn't helpless. He wasn't being pushed. He was moving himself. And the wheelchair wasn't slowing him down. It was speeding him up.

"Oh, I know him," Dexter said. "That's Salim. I think he lives near my cousin Deano. He's supposed to be an amazing basketball player."

It would be amazing to move that fast, I thought. But isn't walking always supposed to be better? I felt really confused and guilty thinking this stuff. It made me want to change the subject, and change it quickly.

"Come on, let's get home and practise a few shots before dinner time," I said. "Spencer might want a rematch."

Dexter put a hand out. Shed, Brian and I did the same, and we all performed the Parsons Road Gang handshake.

"Spencer can do what he likes," Brian said. "Because, together, we're invincible."

"Yes, we are!" we all said as one.

I grinned. The Parsons Road Gang were a team and together, we really were invincible.

# WHAT WILL ADE AND THE PARSONS ROAD GANG GET UP TO NEXT? FIND OUT IN

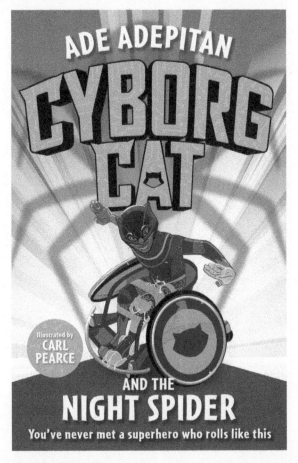

Is Cyborg Cat just a nickname or does Ade truly have superpowers? When the mysterious Night Spider weaves a web of suspense the gang are put to the test ...
*Read on for a sneak peek.*

# 1

# Boing-boing Leopards and Bum-bum Bees

**"WHAT** a save!"

"Incredible!"

"Cyborg Cat is taking his game to superhuman levels! How does he do it?"

My goalkeeping that day was pretty good, if I do say so myself. The Parsons Road gang was playing football after school. I was in goal against Dexter, Melody, Shed and Brian, and I'd saved just

about every one of their shots. Maybe it was because I was in a really good mood – we'd just found out that we were going on a school trip to a safari park. Or perhaps my cyborg skills were growing. Either way, I was on blistering form.

"Your super-cyborg leg was practically glowing when you made that last save," Dexter shouted, wide-eyed and out of breath. "I'm telling you, the caliper is the source of his powers," Brian said seriously.

The gang looked in awe at the metal scaffolding surrounding my left leg. I'd contracted polio in Nigeria when I was six, which made my leg weak, so it was there to help me walk. But it had earned me the nickname Cyborg Cat amongst my friends because I could do cool moves no one ever expected. The element of surprise was my secret weapon on the football pitch.

"Er, guys!" I said, feeling a little awkward. "I'm still here, you know. I can actually hear what you're saying."

"Sorry, Ade, but we're never going to score against you today," said Shed. "I reckon even a team of animals from the safari park wouldn't be able to get a goal past the Cyborg Cat."

That got me thinking.

What a pass by Lenny Lion, straight to Eric Elephant who controls the ball and back heels it to Terry Tiger. Terry beats one beast, beats two, beats a third and sends in a beautiful cross. Geoffrey Giraffe out-jumps the defenders and heads it perfectly ... it must be a goal, surely ... but no! Cyborg Cat launches himself through the air, stretches out and somehow tips the ball over the bar. How did he do that? He must have super-powers!

Dexter was talking as I came out of my daydream. "I've never been to a safari park before, it's going to be amazing!" he said excitedly. Melody picked up the ball and the five of us started heading back to Parson's Road.

"Yeah, I can't wait! This could be the Parson's Road gang's greatest adventure ever," chipped in Brian. "I'm going to research all the animals and make notes on them all, with drawings, diagrams, charts and everything."

I looked at Shed and shook my head. Sometimes it seemed as if Brian was more interested in making notes than the actual thing he was making notes about.

"I really hope we see the *Equus quagga*," Brian went on, seemingly in a world of his own. "And the odd-toed ungulate from the well-known *Rhinocerotidae* family. And I definitely reckon we'll see the ferocious *Panthera leo*."

Everyone looked at Brian strangely.

"You're speaking Bri-brainium again," Melody said, with a sigh.

This was the name Melody gave to the language she reckoned Brian spoke when he got super-excited about something.

"I think it's Latin, Melody," I said. "At least that's what my dad said, when he heard it."

"I know Latin," Dexter replied confidently. "My cousin used to live there, it's the stop after Stratford on the Central Line."

"That's Leyton, Dex!" I replied, trying not to laugh.

Brian gave Melody a look, then turned to rest of us shaking his head. "I was talking about the animals in the safari park. *Equus quagga* is also known as the zebra, *Rhinocerotudae* is the rhino, and *Panthera leo* is the lion."

"OHHHH! Well, obvs!" shouted Dexter. "Why didn't you just say that in the first place? I can do all of them."

He dropped on all-fours and gave us his best impressions of a zebra, rhino and lion, as well as a giraffe and a warthog. Apparently. They all just seemed to involve crawling and grunting, but he did look funny doing it.

Brian wasn't impressed.

"Your warthog is exactly the same as your giraffe," he said. "Which is exactly the same as your zebra, lion and rhino."

"No, it isn't," objected Dexter, demonstrating again for Brian's benefit.

"Afraid it is, Dex," said Shed. "Hey, Ade, tell Dexter the difference between a warthog and a giraffe."

Why would Shed think I knew? I looked at him and made a face that I hoped said, *Eh? What on earth are you talking about, mate?*

Shed got it and replied, "Well, you must be an expert because you'll have seen them all in Africa when you lived there, Ade."

"Yeah," said Brian. "He's got a point. You probably know loads of cool stuff that I could add to my research."

I looked at my friends. They were the best mates anyone could ever have, but sometimes they could be really dense. I mean, *really* dense. Even Brian. So much so that I was going to tell them that I was hardly an expert and I knew as much about animals as they all did about flower arranging, when I stopped. I grinned to myself. This was the perfect opportunity for a wind-up.

"I am an expert, in fact," I said, holding my head up high and trying to look as expertly expert as I could. "My village in Nigeria was always full of animals. There were two-headed emus and giant spotted flying camels all over the place, they were practically my pets."

By the time I'd finished describing

these mystical beasts, I was in full David Attenborough mode.

Dexter's eyes were as big as snooker balls, and his mouth had opened so wide in amazement at the thought of these incredible animals that I'm sure I caught a glimpse of the gooey Wagon Wheel he'd scoffed for lunch. I desperately tried to keep a straight face as I carried on.

"Oh, and my personal favourite are the bum-bum bees. They're half bee and half bottom! They feed exclusively on baked beans. You always know when they're near because of the terrible stench and the sound."

"Bum-bum bees?" Dexter said quizzically. "What sound do they make?"

I leant over in his direction, pursed my lips together and *Pffffffffffffffffffffffffffff!* I blew a large raspberry in his ear.

"They're basically like a swarm of

giant flying farts," I said, when I was all
raspberried out. "Just a whiff of their odour
is enough to kill a fully grown human!"

Brian and Melody obviously weren't fooled,
and Shed shook his head with amusement,
but Dexter bought it hook, line and sinker.

"Two-headed emus, giant spotted flying
camels and bum-bum bees? I can't wait to
see them!" he shouted.

Brian and Shed fell about laughing. Even
Melody was giggling.

"What? What is it?"

"Dex," I said. "If you ever see a bum-bum

bee or a giant flying camel I'm taking you straight to the doctor."

Dexter looked cross when he realized I'd been teasing him. "Yeah, well, what if I see a night spider?" he said defiantly.

That *really* wasn't what I'd expected him to say.

Dexter was pointing to a wall with the coolest graffiti I'd ever seen. We all looked up at it. There was a splash of colourful zig-zags interspersed with googly eyes and sparkly diamonds. At the bottom the artist

had signed it: Night Spider. The 'N' and the 'S' were much bigger and brighter than the other letters so they really stood out.

"Wow, cool," said Melody.

"Amazing," I agreed. "I wonder who this Night Spider is?"

My question was greeted by silence. The gang just stared at the wall, blown away by the Night Spider's work. But there was something about the graffiti that made me feel weird and uneasy. I looked at the others. They were all acting normally, pointing out their favourite bits to each other, but something strange was happening to me, I could feel it. Suddenly my caliper started glowing a dull orange.

"What's happening?" I muttered under my breath.

The rest of the gang didn't seem to notice. I looked back at the graffiti and the colours started swirling around me like a rainbow.

# SCHWOOOOM!

I gasped as I felt myself being sucked into the bright, spray-painted swirls.

*No way!* I thought, my mind struggling to understand what was happening. I was floating through the air, with unfamiliar images all around me. *Is this real?* I wondered.

Then I heard a strange shuffling sound.

"Hello, Cyborg Cat," a low whispy voice said.

I spun in the air like an astronaut floating in outer space, searching for who was speaking.

Who said that? Why did they call me Cyborg Cat?

My caliper began to glow even brighter than before and I felt myself getting drawn deeper and deeper into the graffiti. The colours became more intense and I felt as if I was melting into them.

"It's nice to meet you," said the voice.

"Where am I?" I asked. "What is this world?"

But instead of an answer I heard...

"Ade! Are you okay? Are you okay, Ade?"

This voice sounded distant, but familiar. It took me a few seconds to recognise it.

"Oi, you sausage, what are you doing?"

It was Melody. Her stern but friendly question had released me from the grip of the graffiti. My brain quickly jumped back to reality and I let out a loud sigh of relief.

"What's going on, Ade? You looked like you were dreaming."

Melody was right. Something strange had happened to me. Cold sweat dripped down my back. I realised I was shaking.

"Are you sure you're okay, Ade?" Shed asked, giving me a concerned look.

"Didn't you guys see that? Didn't you hear the voice?"

"What voice?" they all replied in unison.

I stared back at the gang, totally confused. Was I really the only one who had gone inside the graffiti?

"The voice of the NIGHT SPIDER!" I shouted.

"AHH! I get it," Dexter exclaimed. "Did the Night Spider have a tail, twelve legs and eyes the size of snooker balls?" He looked at Melody, Brian and Shed with a satisfied smirk on his face.

"Apart from the tail and the four extra legs that's probably a pretty good description, Dex," I said seriously. "But I didn't see it. I just heard it."

"You heard the Night Spider talking?" replied Melody, staring at me like I'd lost my mind. "You do have a vivid imagination, Ade."

Shed put one of his big meaty arms around my shoulders.

"Come on, you lot, all this Night Spider

talk is freaking me out," he said, trying to change the subject. "Let's get home."

I sighed. Maybe Melody was right and it was just my imagination.

"Well, I believe you, Ade," Dexter said as we got closer to home. "What if the Night Spider is a superhero, like you're the Cyborg Cat? You could team up and fight evil villains."

"Well," said Shed. "I'd rather be a cyborg cat than a night spider. No one can leap through the air and make saves like you, Ade, when you're in super cyborg-cat mode."

"Hey," said Brian, "I wonder if there'll be a cyborg cat at the safari park?"

"No chance," said Shed. "Ade's the one and only Cyborg Cat."

If only they believed me about what had happened with the wall. Maybe Cyborg Cat wasn't just a nickname after all? But I decided I'd better not mention it again. I didn't want them to think I was weird.

"Yeah," I said. "Lions are rubbish goalkeepers."

"So if Cyborg Cat isn't a lion, what is he?" said Brian. "'Cause I think he's a jaguar."

"Nah," said Melody. "Cyborg Cat is definitely a panther."

"You're both wrong," I told them assertively. "When I'm Cyborg Cat I'm a boing-boing leopard, that's one with springs in its feet, so it bounces everywhere. There were loads in Africa."

"Wow, I can't wait to see ..." Dexter stopped. This time he realised I was joking, and we all fell about laughing again anyway.

After saying goodbye to Melody, who lived on a different street, we continued messing about all the way to Parson's Road. We were just tiptoeing past Mr Collins' house, so as not to wake King, his large and very excitable German Shepherd, when we heard ...

"Hey, you lot – catch!"

Salim hurtled past in his wheelchair, having just lobbed a basketball in our direction.

"Incoming!" shouted Brian.

"I've got it!" I yelled.

I lunged forward to catch the ball just before it hit Shed's head. Then I hurled it straight back to Salim, who caught it perfectly on the move and swung back round to face us. Salim played for the Newham Rollers, a wheelchair basketball team, and it turned out he was good friends with Melody so we'd seen him around quite a bit over the summer.

"Nice throw, Ade," he said. "You been practising?"

"Nah, just got the gift, haven't I?" I replied, grinning, and opening my front door. "See you tomorrow, guys."

# 2
# An Alarming Incident

**"MUM,** do you remember the colobus monkeys that used to play in the trees near Gran Gran's house?" I asked, as I shovelled cereal into my mouth at breakfast the next morning.

"Of course I do, Doyin," said Mum. "Why are you asking that?"

Mum and Dad always call me by the other half of my full name, Adedoyin. But I prefer Ade, it seems to fit in better in England, somehow.

"Brian, Shed and Dexter think I must be an animal expert because I lived in Africa."

"I see," said Mum. "Well, what else do you remember about Gran Gran's?"

I stopped mid-shovel, a large pile of cornflakes hovering just in front of my face, and thought for a moment.

"I remember me and Olumide, Femi, Neeke and Toyin would try to creep really slowly up to the trees to get a better look at the monkeys, but just as we got close Toyin would shout, 'Monkey!' and scare them away." It used to drive us crazy, I remembered, but Toyin was the youngest of my cousins, and she was only four, I suppose.

Mum smiled. I could tell she was thinking about it as well.

"And I can remember Gran Gran hollering, 'Doyin!' and then we'd know it was time for lunch," I went on. "She'd make all our favourites – jollof rice, fried plaintain, moi

moi. I can smell it now, it was delicious!"

"It was," said Mum, and for a moment she seemed to drift away, as if she was back in Nigeria herself. I knew Mum missed Gran Gran as much as I did. Even though we were settling in on Parsons Road, Mum certainly hadn't forgotten her family.

"Ehh, hehh!" she said suddenly in her strong Nigerian accent, snapping out of it. "So yes, there were some animals like the colobus monkeys, but not all over the place and certainly not in Lagos where we lived. So I'm not sure you could really say you're an animal expert, Doyin! Now finish your breakfast and get ready for school."

Ten minutes later I was hurrying up Parsons Road. We were late and I was struggling to keep up with the boys. My leg had been hurting all morning and the caliper felt heavier than usual.

Shed looked worried. He could see I wasn't my normal energetic self.

"Do you want me to help you?" he asked sympathetically.

"No!" I snapped angrily.

As soon as I said it I felt bad. I knew he was only trying to help, but I didn't want to show any weakness, not even in front of my friends. After all, I was the Cyborg Cat. Shed looked slightly embarrassed, and slumped off.

"Is it your polio again?" Dexter asked, looking me up and down as I limped on.

Trust Dexter to get straight to the point.

Mum said I was about fifteen months old when I caught polio. My temperature was so high I almost died and I was rushed to hospital and put in intensive care. The next morning, when I woke up, the doctors told

Mum and Dad the disease had destroyed all the muscles in my left leg so I would have to wear a caliper. It's a set of iron rods that go down each side of my leg, before slotting into holes in the sides of my hospital boot. The caliper replaces the muscles that I don't have and helps me to put weight on my leg so I can walk. I only took it off when I went to bed. When I was younger I used to hate wearing it, because it made me walk with a limp. But now I'm the Cyborg Cat and my caliper gives me strength!

"Nah, I'm okay, Dex," I replied quickly. "I'm just a bit knackered. I couldn't sleep last night thinking about the school trip."

"Yeah, it's going to be so cool!" Dex answered, satisfied that I was okay.

We caught up with Shed and Brian, still chatting about the safari park trip, but soon it was mainly Brian doing the talking. He'd started his research and was telling us about the feeding habits of warthogs and how they kneel down to eat. To be honest, it was a bit like we were at school already, so I was pretty relieved when we turned a corner and saw something that stopped Brian in his tracks.

"Wow, look at this!" shouted Dexter. "It's even better than the other one."

He was right about that. In front of us was more spectacular Night Spider graffiti. This one was an incredible scene of spiders and insects, all surfing on a huge wave. At the bottom once again was the Night Spider's tag.

'N, S, N, S. Who could that be?" said Shed.

We all gawped at the Night Spider's new masterpiece, but as the boys took a closer look, I made sure to stay back. The graffiti was truly spellbinding, but I wasn't going to make the same mistake as I did yesterday. I was taking no chances about getting sucked into it again.

"Ade, what are you doing?" Brian said, laughing out loud.

Dexter and Shed turned to look at me and immediately started laughing as well.

I guess I must have looked odd standing sideways on to the wall and looking at it out of the corner of my eye, but I was hoping that if I didn't stare at it full-on then I would be protected. I still

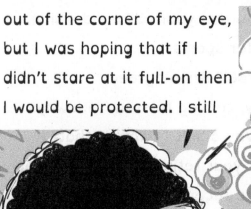

couldn't understand why I was the only one affected by the weird power of the graffiti.

"Yeah, why are you giving the wall the side-eye, Ade?" Shed asked.

"Can't believe you don't know," I said thinking quickly. "Standing sideways is supposed to improve your all-round vision. It's very good for sports."

"Yes, of course!" Brian agreed enthusiastically, coming to stand sideways next to me. "Why didn't I think of that? It must stimulate your retina and improve your peripheral vision receptors."

"Uhh?" Dexter and Shed gave Brian a strange look. I'd made the whole story up, and even I started to wonder what he was talking about.

They came over to stand next to me as well, though. I was glad no one else came along. The four of us standing there facing each other, while also trying to look at the graffiti sideways, must have looked very strange.

"All these insects are making me think of the Creepy Crawly house at the safari park," said Dexter. "It's meant to be really scary. My brother said when he went there, three children got eaten by a giant Praying Mantis."

We all looked at Dex.

"But I knew he was joking, of course."

"Yeah, yeah, Dex," I said, starting to run towards school. "Come on, we're going to be late."

I heard Brian say, "But I haven't told you about warthogs' eyesight yet."

Lucky escape!

"Okay, everyone," said Mr Hurst. "Put your permission slips for the safari park trip on my desk and then line up by the door."

I patted my pocket just to check the slip

was still in there and stood up. Everyone in the class was going on the trip so there was a bit of a crush at Mr Hurst's desk, but eventually I made it to the front and put the precious piece of paper down on top of all the others. I headed over to the line and found myself behind the last person I wanted to stand next to: Spencer. He'd taken an instant dislike to me on my very first day at school and things hadn't got any better since. I guess Spencer and his mates had never got over losing to the Parson's Road Gang at football in front of the whole school. He thought my caliper would slow me down, but he underestimated its cyborg super-skills.

"I'll be surprised if they let you and your mates out of the safari park," he hissed. "You're as stupid as most of the animals there and twice as ugly."

"Yeah, well, they probably won't even let you in ... Neville," I replied.

That really riled him. We'd only recently found out that Spencer was in fact his middle name. His first name was Neville, which for some reason he hated. I couldn't understand why. A name like Adedoyin made me stand out a bit too much, but I thought Neville was actually a pretty cool name. Anyway, Spencer hated it and so it was great ammunition. Whenever Spencer tried anything nasty, a quick reminder was all it took to get him really cheesed off.

"Don't you call me that, you freak," is what I think he said back to me, but it was drowned out by a loud bell.

# Driiiinnnngggg!
# Driiiinnnngggg!
# Driiiinnnngggg!

"Fire alarm drill," Mr Hurst shouted above the ringing. "Make your way down the stairs and out to the meeting place quickly, but in an orderly fashion."

Dexter hared past me shouting, 'Out of my way, future World Cup winner coming through!' I could tell that this was going to be anything but orderly.

As the rest of the class headed out I got swept along and found myself being pushed, bumped and jostled from all sides. At first it was quite a laugh, like being inside a huge wobbly jelly, but as the tide of kids swept me along I realised it was actually the perfect opportunity to practise my Cyborg Cat caliper skills. Even though I'd felt tired all morning, I was hoping the excitement would kick start my powers.

"Come on, caliper, a little help please!!"

I probably looked even stranger than usual pleading with my leg as I tried to keep up with the rowdy crowd charging out, and then ...

**THHUUUDD!**

I had the wind knocked out of me by one of Spencer's mates barging into my back as he flew past.

"OUT OF THE WAY, PEG LEG BOY!" he shouted mockingly.

I started to lose my balance. I stretched my arms out, hoping to find something to hold on to. At best this was going to be mega-awkward, at worst super-embarrassing.

Suddenly, though, everything started to move in slow motion. It was as if somebody had pressed an action replay button in my head and I could anticipate every move milliseconds before it happened.

Without hesitation I turned my fall into an athletic forward roll, finishing in a Cyborg Cat crouch, with arms out by my sides like I was a bird about to fly, my right knee bent and my caliper leg stretched out.

It was like the feeling I'd had inside the graffiti wall. As if I'd discovered a new

dimension. Had I turned into Cyborg Cat for a few moments?

"Wow!" gasped a group of girls who had seen what had happened. I snapped back to the real world, looked over in their direction and winked.

Shed caught my eye and grinned. When he'd first met me he'd assumed my caliper would stop me doing a lot of things, but when he saw me leaping through the air to make great saves he realised the exact opposite was true. The Parsons Road Gang had given me my nickname, Cyborg Cat, because of it. The kids who'd seen my forward roll were having the same realization.

With my confidence high and my powers kicking in, I started to glide through the crowds of screaming students, picking up speed all the time.

"How the – ?" shouted someone as I raced past him with my unique style of awkward agility.

"Woo-hoo!" yelled Dexter from somewhere up ahead.

By now I was in full Cyborg Cat mode, using my caliper to slide along the floor and

then
stopping
suddenly to
change direction with
a really cool crunching
sound.

"Wait for me!" shouted Brian, almost
totally out of breath.

There was no way I was slowing down,
though. At the top of the stairs
I began weaving through the crowd as if I
was skiing. Then, halfway down, I had what I
thought was a great idea.

I decided it would be faster, and a lot more
fun, to hop onto the banister and slide to the

bottom on my caliper. So I did.

"Slow down, Ade, you're going too fast," I heard Melody shouting, as she tried to hold back her laughter.

"Oh dear, this is going to end very badly! I can feel it in my bones," said Brian, still trying to keep up.

I was having trouble getting a clear shot at it, though.

"Out of the way everybody, Cyborg Cat coming through!" Shed ordered from behind me.

Perhaps the other kids thought he was a teacher.

Or maybe he just had the sort of commanding voice that people listened to. Whatever it was, my path cleared and my route to the bottom seemed easy.

At least it would have been if I hadn't suddenly lost my balance and tumbled off the banister. "OOOHH! NOO!"

As I fell, I heard Dexter shouting at the top of his voice. "Don't worry! Cats have nine lives! Long live Cyborg Caaaaaat!"

I hit the ground and screamed as a sharp shooting pain shot up the back of my leg. It was so agonizing it took my breath away. There was no time to worry about my leg or the pain, though. My fall had sent me hurtling onwards into a group of kids at the bottom of the stairs. I crashed into them like a bowling ball and, just like skittles, they went flying.

"Ow!" shouted the first girl I banged into.

"Oof!" went another.

"Ouch!" said a third.

And, "Who did that? I'm going to kill them," said a fourth, all too familiar, voice. It was Spencer. Just my luck.

"Sorry, sorry, sorry," I spluttered, stretching out to pick up the scattered books, pencil cases, rulers and sharpeners all around me on the floor.

The girl who'd said 'Ow' was glaring at me and holding her arm.

"Are you okay?" I asked, looking up at her from where I was lying. And then, because I couldn't think of anything else to say, "Sorry, sorry, sorry," again.

"Of course she's not okay," snapped Spencer, standing over me. "None of us are okay, you stupid cripple."

"Yeah, let's get him," said the person who'd said 'Oof'.

"No, really, it was an accident," I pleaded, still on the floor. "I didn't mean it."

"Yeah, and I don't mean this," said Spencer curling his hand into a fist. "Stand up and face me, you freak."

This was serious. I was still in a lot of pain and I was pretty sure my leg would give way if I tried to stand up. My Cyborg Cat powers were drained, there was no way out.

"No, you don't. Back off, Spencer. There are two of us."

It was Shed. He'd seen what was going on and, in the true spirit of the Parson's Road Gang, had come to help me.

"It's still four against two," spat Spencer.

"Three," said another voice. It was Brian.

"Make that four," said Melody, appearing behind Spencer.

"Actually, make that thirteen!" said another voice confidently.

Everybody looked around in confusion, to see Dexter counting his fingers and doing calculations in his head. He explained to

Spencer that as Cyborg Cat had eight lives left, and there were five of us, eight plus five equals thirteen.

"Moron!" spat Spencer, before turning his attentions back to me. "Get up, you loser!"

"I was only trying to help," said Dexter, looking at me apologetically and shrugging his shoulders.

"Here, Ade," said Shed holding out an arm to help me up.

I was just about to grab it when Mrs Lincoln, the deputy headteacher, turned up.

"What on earth is going on here?" she shouted. "You'd have all been burnt to a crisp by now if this had been a real fire. Pick up all this rubbish and get outside now!"

"But, miss, it wasn't our fault," said Spencer. "It was him." He pointed at me.

"Yeah," said the 'oof' kid.

"He broke my arm," said the girl.

"Enough!" shouted Mrs Lincoln. "You are

ALL in detention. Outside, now!"

Detention? I knew everyone would be very angry with me. They trudged off outside, but I knew that there was no way I could get up.

"You too, Ade," said Mrs Lincoln. "Now."

"I ... I can't, miss," I said. "I can't stand up."

Suddenly Mrs Lincoln changed from being strict and teacherly to very concerned indeed.

"Okay, okay, just stay there, Ade. I'm going to get the school nurse and then I'll call your parents. Will you be all right there for a couple of minutes?"

"Yes, I'll be fine," I said, out loud. In my head, I added: *I'm going nowhere.*

*Cyborg Cat
and the Night Spider*
will be available from all places
good books are sold.

Find out more about Ade Adepitan
and what he's up to at
**adeadepitan.com**

Thank you for choosing a Piccadilly Press book.

If you would like to know more about our authors, our books or if you'd just like to know what we're up to, you can find us online.

**www.piccadillypress.co.uk**

You can also find us on:

**We hope to see you soon!**